OFFICE MUTANT

PETE RISLEY

GRINDHOUSE
PRESS

Grindhouse Press
PO BOX 293161
Dayton, Ohio 45429

Grindhouse Press # 035
ISBN-10: 1-941918-25-5
ISBN-13: 978-1-941918-25-8

This is a work of fiction. All characters and events portrayed in this book are fictitious and any resemblance to real people or events is purely coincidental.

Other titles by Pete Risley

Rabid Child
The Toehead

In Memory of Lulu

1.

The alarm clock howled, provoking the bed into so violent a spasm that its inhabitant, Timothy Plummet, was thrown half-way across the room. After hitting the floor, he tumbled a short distance and ended in a sprawl, face up in the center of a beam of morning sunlight shining in from the window above him. He winced, but didn't move. The alarm kept ringing.

An eternity passed.

Finally, with obvious pain, he raised his head from the floor. A whine escaped his throat. His eyes attempted to crawl from their dark and cavernous sockets, but were driven back by the cruel sun.

His head fell back to the floor with a thud. The alarm kept ringing.

Tim's wince became a full grimace. He trembled, apparently

from an extreme effort to hold himself perfectly still. His toes curled, the big toe on his left foot producing a popping sound.

The alarm took on an oddly heightened quality in his mind. It was no longer just an irritating sound, but an oppressive presence, an entity with a visual aspect as well as an aural one. It swirled violently before his closed eyes, a montage of fragments from uncountable unremembered dreams, pouring out like the plagues in Pandora's box, as if from a hole in his head.

The dream fragments blurred as they rose into the air, becoming blue, red and yellow blotches on the walls and ceiling of the bedroom. Then, for the sheerest moment, they reshaped into perfectly round spots.

Upon attaining perfect roundness, the spots disappeared though the alarm kept ringing, as obstinately as before.

Then came another sound: a loud rapping, followed by a familiar voice.

"Tim, you're up, aren't you?"

The speaker was Betty, Tim's wife. She stood outside the bedroom door. She was always up and about in the mornings before him.

"Yes, of course I am, dear," he said clearly and pleasantly though he was still splayed out on the floor. "I was just getting ready to come downstairs."

The alarm rang on. Betty apparently had stepped away, for she said nothing more.

Lying there, still submerged in a quicksand of inertia, despair swept through him. He knew his entire life was going wrong, though he hadn't allowed himself to contemplate the matter when he was fully in possession of himself. He was losing control. Every morning it was worse, every Monday morning especially. The arrangement just wasn't working the way he'd hoped it would. The chaos out there in the world at large was creeping into his home, his private domain, the place in which he was supposed to be king. But no, he didn't want to think about it—mustn't, couldn't, wouldn't let it preoccupy him—and his rising determination not to do so brought him almost fully awake.

He painfully forced his eyes open and dragged himself to his feet. He stumbled over to the dresser and seized the alarm clock with both hands. Its cry took on a note of terror as he pounded it into submission.

Tim put on his glasses and got dressed in an aggravated frenzy. He had lain on the floor too long and would now be late for work. Betty had laid out his clothes for the day, as always, on the chair near his bed. Stripping out of his polka dot nightshirt, he put on his underwear, his suit pants, his stiff-ironed white shirt and his suit jacket, and hung his tie around his neck. When he got to his socks, he was struck with dread, and the despair threatened to engulf him once again.

The socks didn't match. One was black and the other dark blue. Further, the dark blue one had a rather sizable hole in its heel.

He put them on anyway, scrunching the bad sock down so its hole wouldn't show at the back of his heel. He didn't have time to complain to Betty about it now. Besides, in his present queasy state, that might be dangerous. He would do so this evening, when he would surely feel stronger.

He rushed to the bathroom, turned on the sink's faucets, and splashed water onto his face. He had no time to bathe, let alone shave. Fortunately, his beard was light, though that was also why his carefully cultivated moustache tended so often to curl upward at one side, as it was doing now.

He was still knotting his tie as he hurried down the stairs. Betty stood at the bottom, in her apron. Her deportment appalled him, for she wasn't smiling, and her hair was a terrible unruly mess. However, he chose not to say anything about it.

"Breakfast is ready, dear," she said, a bit forlornly, Tim thought.

"I really don't have time for it," he replied, brushing past her.

"But Tim, you're already late. It will only take a minute. I really don't know why it took you so long to get up, but I have gone to the trouble—"

"Thank you dear, no," said Tim, as firmly as he could manage. He pulled his coat from the living room closet, grabbed his briefcase, and plunked his hat on his head. He glanced, in passing, at the large framed painting hanging on the living room wall—antlers, rainbow—and then at the twins, Clark and Shirley, sitting in the kitchen at the table and staring at him. "See you this evening, dear."

"I could put your coffee in a thermos, at least," said Betty.

"No," said Tim, stepping through the front door, closing it decisively and setting down his briefcase so he could put his coat on. He hurried over to the garage and pulled up the rattling door.

The horses were waiting inside, as always. At the sight of him they snorted and whinnied, raring to go. Tim scurried behind them and strapped himself into his leather harness. He made sure the reins were secure and situated himself, sitting on the ground in a relatively comfortable position for skidding.

He snapped the reins expertly, and the horses galloped off,

dragging Tim behind them. They turned out of the driveway and into the street, picking up speed and raising a great cloud of dust, especially around Tim himself.

He shifted to his left side as his right buttock began to burn. Friction was always a problem, and the horses were feisty today.

The horses galloped on at a good clip. They came to a red light and stopped along with the rest of the traffic. Waiting out the light, Tim squirmed impatiently. He hoped he wouldn't catch too many red lights. He was late enough already.

Someone from the neighborhood, a fellow Tim didn't know very well but saw occasionally at the local bowling alley, though he was on a different bowling team than Tim's, sat in his car at the next lane. Just before the light changed to green, the man looked over at Tim and cautiously lifted his hand from the steering wheel to wave hello. Tim nodded back as the light changed, smiling as best he could as the horses took off again and he began to skid. It was hard to act friendly on Monday mornings, especially just lately.

After catching four more red lights and running the last with nearly disastrous results, Tim finally arrived at the massive, dark-hued Bureau of Verification building where he was employed. He extricated himself from his harness and, straightening his bedraggled and dusty jacket, sent the horses on their way.

He used the back entrance of the building as usual but, when he got inside, found to his displeasure the door of the elevator he always took covered with a sheet of heavy plastic, and taped to it was a sign which read:

OUT OF ORDER DUE TO REPAIRS

He sighed dispiritedly. He might as well have used the front entrance. Now he'd have to take the elevators in the lobby and walk past the claimants.

Then came the first trace of the dreaded Smell but, fortunately, no glimmer of the Spots. Perhaps there wouldn't be any today, despite his dream that morning. The Smell occurred more frequently than the Spots. He suspected both were the result of simply thinking about them and expecting them. The Smell, oddly mutable, though usually as now beginning as a faint trace of sweet rot, was more frequent, perhaps because it was less alarming and distracting. He hurried down the corridor, dusting off his pants as he went and thinking in his practiced manner: it's alright, don't be so negative, don't think about it, no, don't let it in, keep it out, don't think at all, just cheerful, think positively...

The other elevator banks were just across the hall from the entrance to the Certification of Inquiries Department, which took up the entire first floor. Masses of people would report there every day to file appeals of various kinds when the determinations on their claims hadn't come out the way they had hoped, in many cases with some desperation. On Monday mornings the place was always crowded and tense, as Tim well knew from having worked in that department some years before.

As he rounded a corner into the lobby, he saw that, though appointments didn't begin for almost another hour, a number of claimants were already assembled outside the door, anxious and impatient, many of them rather scroungy-looking by Tim's judgment and, some of them, he sensed, in fairly dangerous moods. All the worse, there were no other staff persons around.

He made for the elevators and pressed the up button, carefully keeping his back turned to the line of claimants, as he didn't want any of them to try and get his attention.

Behind him, he heard a couple of them talking.

"Man, these people work here ain't shit, you know? They act like they all better than you, and you asking them for somethin' outa their pocket. You s'posed to be here right on time, then they keep your ass standin' 'round three hour or some shit. I been waitin' six fuggin' weeks since my *request* got put in, and now they tell me I gotta file it all over, start all over, 'cause some asswipe upstairs lose the file!"

"That's ridiculous!" came another, deeper voice, amid cluck-ings and sympathetic murmurs from the rest of the claimants present. "You should write your congressman over that shit."

Tim pressed the button again, pulled his arm back and held very still. Come on, elevator, please!

"Congressman *shit*! I told them I want the *name* of that fuggin' asswipe. I want the fuggin' *name* and *address*. I talk to the sumbitch my own self and ask him how I'm s'posed to feed my fuggin' family for six more fuggin' weeks on account of him losin' my fuggin' file, *goddammit!* I mean, I ain't yellin' at you, man, you know."

"I hear ya," came another voice, "these people just be l'il clerks an' shit, they act like they're doin' you a favor just talkin' to you."

"They're *little* shits, man! Check that dude out!"

At that moment, a maintenance man stepped in front of Tim and started staple-gunning a sheet of heavy plastic over the elevator door nearest him. Wasn't that bad for the plaster, thought Tim, but what he said to the man was:

"They're all out?"

"All what?" replied the maintenance man, without turning.

"The elevators," said Tim. "I see that the one by the back is—"

The maintenance man made a slight directional gesture with his head. "Stairs still work."

Suppressing a whimper, Tim walked, briskly but not so fast as to appear to be hurrying, past the line of claimants to the staircase on the other side of the lobby. As he went by he glanced up to see, prominent among the clustered group, a tall young man with a stubbly beard and blond bangs in his eyes, wearing a t-shirt which failed to cover the belly hanging out over his jeans and beneath his thick folded arms. At the young man's side was a heavy-set black man in a workshirt and a dingy baseball cap, and both of them, along with the entire line of claimants, watched Tim with faces like clenched fists.

"Hey, sir," said the blond man, whose face was clenched the tightest and whose voice was the angry one Tim had first heard. "Mind if I ask ya a question?"

"Sorry, I've gotta . . ." said Tim, stepping faster and finishing his sentence by gesturing at the staircase. He reached it and began ascending rapidly, taking two steps at each leap. Some of the claimants began laughing.

"Hey, buddy! Hey!"

They were laughing louder, but Tim was through the door on the first landing, which led to the second staircase. Not following, is he? No. Whew! Tim had been lucky to avoid a situation there that might have resulted in an Incident Report. Of course, when that happened the Bureau always blamed it on you rather than on the scummy claimants. Well, thank goodness he didn't have to work in Cert Ink anymore.

Tim's office was five flights up, but he didn't mind the exertion so much. What did worry him, right at the moment, was that he would now have to walk past the office of the department manager, Mr. Grovel, who was sometimes rather moody, to put it mildly, and who probably wouldn't be pleased to see Tim arriving for work about—he checked his watch—twenty minutes late. The rear elevator would have let him off on the opposite side of the floor. Well, he would just have to hope for the best, step quietly and try not to be noticed.

He huffed up all five flights and walked briskly past Grovel's office. He was pleased to see, from the corner of his eye, that it was unoccupied except for Grovel's lovely young secretary, Dora, who was typing busily as usual. Perhaps, he mused, Mr. Grovel was already relaxing over at his favorite hangout, a little tavern a block from the office called The Wee Nippy, though on most days he didn't go there until almost noon.

It was well known in the office Mr. Grovel did this, and no one really blamed him, except for the more malicious employees. After all, Mr. Grovel was less than two years away from retirement and, due to a number of reorganizations, most of his real work had been taken away from him. It was even said his only real function was to serve as a scapegoat and whipping boy for his own higher-ups in the Bureau whenever anything went wrong enough to attract their notice. Thus, it was no wonder he was sometimes short-tempered with some of the staff he had authority over—like Tim, for instance.

Tim's nostrils flexed uncomfortably as he reflected on these matters. Darn! He must have thought about the Smell again without even noticing he had done so.

But maybe there really was a Smell—today, anyway—and it had come from those claimants downstairs. In fact, it had occurred to him more than once they might be the real source of it, though that didn't entirely add up. How could it waft all the way upstairs and, more than that, seem even stronger upstairs than downstairs, sometimes becoming a nauseating stench like that of an open sewer—worse, one would think, than the most unsanitary of claimant mobs could produce on an ordinary day. Could the ventilation system actually make it worse? Besides, though he feared and avoided the claimants whenever possible, he wasn't comfortable thinking such an unpleasant thing about them. It made more sense to conclude the Smell was actually produced by thinking about the Smell, however vaguely and distantly, and by nothing else. Of course, once the Smell emerged, the Spots were usually not far behind. If he could only keep both out of his mind, the problem wouldn't even exist.

The entire sixth floor was a patchwork of offices separated by winding, narrow corridors. In the heart of the jumble of offices was the Preverification Department, housed in a small room filled with an elaborate hive of cubicles, at the heart of which was the Space Saver, a rectangular silver box about the size of a compact automobile, with rounded edges making it resemble an old-fashioned toaster, except it lacked slots at the top for slices of bread. This was where Tim worked. Most of the cubicles were already occupied by his co-workers, bent over their desks with their behinds sticking up unpleasantly and their legs hanging down. This posture, though it looked quite undignified and could be uncomfortable, was necessary because the employees' heads had to be inserted wholly into their desk computer terminals in order for them to access the Space Saver.

This had been the arrangement at Tim's workplace for the last year and a half. It used to be the Preverification Department was housed in an enormous room containing row after row of huge filing cabinets that held paper files for each of the seemingly millions of claimants' cases—nothing could ever be discarded for legal reasons—but the cabinets had been hauled away and were said to be kept in a faraway facility, perhaps in another country. The large room they'd formerly occupied was divided into several by the installation of new walls, and the rest of it was now occupied by a variety of other departments. But the Space Saver allowed employees of the Preverification Department to access the files in a generated milieu nearly identical to the way things had worked before the big change, in that same enormous room. Only at the start of the day were things entirely different.

Tim hurried to his cubicle, though he was quite worried about what he'd be faced with once he tuned into the Space Saver. He glanced over at the huge jutting buttocks of his supervisor, Mrs. Henderson, her head already inserted into her terminal a few cubicles away. She would surely be stern with him about his tardiness, as always. Glumly, he bent over, stretched forward and jabbed his head into the pink plastic flaps of his terminal that, as always, seemed to pull him inside with a gulp. The fit was uncomfortably snug, and just lately he'd been getting a needling sensation at the top of his head, at times, while he was working.

After the usual blue sign-on screen blipped past, along with its welcoming notes of muzak, the office image bloomed up, showing that familiar room with rows of gigantic filing cabinets and employees busily digging through them, or poring over files at their desks or talking on telephones. The basic difference from before was everything now was cleaner and bore a slightly unnatural gleam and, perhaps, the filing cabinets looked somewhat bigger. Looking around him, Tim saw his supervisor Mrs. Henderson standing nearby, speaking to his co-worker Sue Frisky. Mrs. Henderson was a squarely built iron-haired woman in her sixties who had worked for the Bureau for a long time and was very devoted to her job.

Well, he might as well go over and speak to her, rather than wait for her to come over to him. She was always crankier when he let things happen that way, though his other concern was she might be more stern with him than otherwise with Sue standing there as an audience.

Tim flipped out of his seat and approached the two women, busily composing his excuse in his head: I'm terribly sorry Mrs. Henderson, my alarm clock didn't wake me up on time, didn't go off at all, have it fixed now and it won't happen again I don't think, I'm sure, I'm sorry, I'll make sure it doesn't continue to be a, I've taken care of the problem . . . He hated situations like this and was actually feeling a bit lightheaded, but perhaps that was because he'd just entered the Space Saver milieu. He was getting that needling sensation again, and Mrs. Henderson and Sue seemed to waver a bit as he approached.

Mrs. Henderson glanced at him momentarily, pausing in mid-sentence while speaking to Sue, but turned her eyes away briskly, as though he were an insignificant sight. He stood there as the two of them rattled on in the shorthand of office jargon, speaking of forms that required the prior completion and approval of other forms, of inadequately presented information that needed to be reevaluated and sent back to an earlier stage of the preverification process, and under what circumstances this could be properly done, what forms needed to be completed, approved and attached, and what determinations made under the authority of what accredited staff-persons. As always, alas, the more one looked into these matters concerning claims, the more complicated and uncertain they became. That was why, in Tim's view, it was better to aim for a reasonable level of complexity and once that had been reached, to be satisfied, to pass it along and go on to the next one.

At any rate, here today, he caught little of what the two of them were saying and only waited, politely and patiently.

Abruptly, the conversation seemed to be over, and Mrs. Henderson had turned her full attention upon Tim, speaking coldly.

"I'm so glad you're finally here, Timothy. We have so much work to do and were terribly worried we'd be short-handed again today."

"Good gracious yes," put in Sue, addressing Mrs. Henderson, "the way some people have been slacking off lately, you'd swear we didn't have any work to do around here."

Tim chose to ignore Sue's comments. "I'm very sorry to be late, but I had a, a problem with my alarm clock this morning, and I . . ."

Sue snorted out a laugh. "A problem with his alarm clock!"

Tim bit the underside of his lip, just slightly, and suppressed a gorge of aggravation that attempted to rise into his throat. Sue Frisky had been working there only a year or so and, in Tim's view, was excessively ambitious and something of a straw boss. She clearly hoped to climb the ladder and become a section manager or something higher, though at present all the middle-management people had their heels dug in pretty deeply and were not planning on retiring or moving on anytime soon. There might be a reorganization when Grovel retired which would open up a position or two, but even that was iffy. Tim doubted that Sue, despite all the performances she put on to try and convince people she was sharp and highly efficient, was really bright enough to figure this out. Further, she'd always made it clear she considered Tim an insignificant person, and so he felt it was appropriate for him to look upon her with a similar attitude.

"Well, I certainly hope that's the case, Timothy," said Mrs Henderson. "Are you sure you wouldn't like me to call you on the telephone every morning to make sure you get up?" Lizard tongues darted from her eyes, behind her rhinestone-studded glasses.

Tim began to apologize, more abjectly than before, when Sue shuffling with the pile of folders which she virtually held, interrupted him.

"Oh, Mrs. Henderson, another thing, I found these on Mr Drivel's desk this morning and I'm very concerned. These are some of those claims Mr. Grovel was concerned about, in which the Supplications board said a Certificate of Tertiary Review would be required before Cert Ink can have them back, but they've been requested anyway and they have the AT71467's completed, but they're from out of that batch where the Moral Aptitude Index findings were found to be consistent with Civil Privileges. Remember when Supps asked us to pull all of those? But with these particular claims, for some reason there was no Certified Evidence of Procedural Completion at the time of the Initial Predetermination . . ."

Mrs. Henderson eyed her archly. "And you found them on Mr. Drivel's desk?"

She flushed slightly though, in the somewhat-off color spectrum of the Space Saver, her cheeks became vaguely red-purple

"I was looking for some other claims, and I just happened upon them. It's a good thing I did though, my goodness! These really require immediate attention. Mr. Grovel was very concerned last time we . . ."

Tim couldn't help but be amused, though he endeavored not to show it. It was rather clear Sue thought she could fulfill her ambitions by criticizing the work of some of her superiors to others of her superiors. This only showed how stupid she really was. Mr. Drivel, whatever his faults, was a full two levels above Mrs. Henderson, who was a devout believer in the sanctity of the organizational hierarchy.

"After all," Sue continued, "the claimants were contracted on a Probational Basis only, with only minimal certification because of the Delay Clause, which became obsolete before the Procedural Review date came up—"

Mrs. Henderson interrupted her. "But wouldn't Mr. Drivel know all that?"

"Well, goodness gracious, he should. I can't imagine how not."

"Have you spoken to him about it?"

"No, I haven't had the chance, I just found them and I thought I should bring them right to you."

"Well, you really should consult with Mr. Drivel about those, Sue, if you have a question about them. He's probably waiting for a response from Administrative Authority. I hope you didn't disrupt Mr. Drivel's desk when you took them away. He may have been keeping them in some specific order with other claims he's busy with. I believe Mr. Drivel is out of the office right now, but I'm sure he'll be back soon. You can ask him about them when he returns."

Sue obviously didn't like this idea at all, but before she could protest, the door to the staff lounge opened. Mr. Drivel, the assistant director of the Bureau, stood in the doorway, his hand on the knob, speaking with great animation to some other staff members in the lounge. He was delivering droll remarks and, as usual, was clearly having a hard time suppressing his own desire to chortle, joining in with the appreciative laughter of the others.

Mr. Drivel was both high up in the office hierarchy and the office clown. Tim had never really found him particularly funny but would laugh along if his co-workers were laughing in situations where it might be noticed if he wasn't. He liked Mr. Drivel well enough, otherwise. He was a fairly nice fellow and never gave Tim, or anyone else, a hard time. Sue Frisky, however, disliked and resented him.

Mr. Drivel could never tear himself away from a responsive audience and was still standing in the doorway and joshing after two or three minutes. Finally Mrs. Henderson called out to him.

"Mr. Drivel? Excuse us please, Mr. Drivel. We have a question for you!"

Mr. Drivel tossed another zinger to the staff lounge crowd, earning more laughs, before shutting the door. He came hurrying over, lifting his knees and elbows in an exaggerated run, causing the carpet to momentarily roll up beneath his feet and gather in bunches behind him, which was odd since the carpet was securely nailed down.

"Yes, ma'am!" he cried. "Present and accounted for!"

"Mr. Drivel," said Mrs. Henderson soberly, "Sue happened to find these claims on your desk—"

"Well, sufferin' succotash! What'd she use, a shovel?"

"—and she had a question about whether a determination

process should have been initiated as of yet, with these."

Sue stood by, looking flustered and only a bit defiant.

Mr. Drivel leafed through the top folder and screwed up his face as though in deep thought. "Hmmmm hmmmmmmmmmmm. Aha! Aha-aha-ahaaaaaaaaaaa!" He shook the folder with vigor and violently stomped his feet, as if squashing something that had fallen out of it. Indeed, springing up out of nowhere from the areas where Drivel stomped were huge, googly-eyed yellow beetles that scampered off crookedly in different directions only to explode moments later in plumes of smoke to the accompaniment of fart-like bleeps.

"Still has a few *bugs* in it, ha ha ha!"

No one laughed along, though Tim would have done so if Sue and Mrs. Henderson had. He wasn't sure whether he himself was the only one who had seen the bugs. Indeed, the Space Saver milieu had occasional glitches like this, with which Tim had grown fairly familiar.

"So they are not at the determination stage as of yet," said Mrs. Henderson, nodding with approval at Mr. Drivel's superior judgment.

"Nope! Not until we make our testimonials! Hi everybody, my name is Ned and I'm a preverificationer!" Again, Mr. Drivel's witticism was greeted with silence.

"Thank you, Mr. Drivel. Please put these back where you found them, Susan. We're waiting for an Administrative Authority investigation to be completed."

Sue slunk off with the batch of folders, and Mr. Drivel, eyeing two of the staffers across the room whom he'd just been entertaining in the lounge, flapped his arms, jumped in the air and, with a burlesque gear-shifting motion, zipped eagerly over to them. Tim had observed before that Drivel didn't like to make jokes and not get laughs. Not certain Mrs. Henderson was finished with him, Tim stood by waiting for further instruction.

"Timothy, I'd appreciate it if you'd go to your desk and get started on some of your work today," said Mrs. Henderson. She turned on her heel and floated busily away.

With a brisk leap, Tim landed back in his chair at his desk. He winced at the disorganized pile of stuff-to-do before him: fat claim folders, memos to be initialed and/or responded to, loose papers that belonged in some of the claim folders, five-layered carbon forms to be filled out and attached to some of those loose papers before they were returned to the claim folders then passed on to the appropriate party. It was funny how Tim could seldom remember on Mondays what he'd been working on the week before until he looked over his desk. In fact, this sometimes happened on Tuesday with Monday's work, and so forth.

The Smell seemed to creep back upon him—or was it? He decided to ignore the possibility in the hope that doing so would make it go away.

As so often, he was uncertain what to do with the claim. He was supposed to, as a Claims Specialist 2, detect matters of question—flaws that is—in the initial assembly of documents preceding the determination stage of a claim, and there was an unspoken expectation he would send a certain number of them back for clarification of issues or, if something was really fishy, onward to the Security & Investigations Department. If he were to approve too many claims without finding matters of question, it might look like he wasn't doing his job. But often, he had to dig pretty deep to find something. Also, he had to be careful not to offend his co-workers by finding flaws in their work, especially those who were in a position to get back at him.

His mind wandered. There were no windows in the office to drift over to and gaze out of, none except inside his own head. Through one such window, he stared with blank longing and fascination at Grovel's secretary, Dora. Though she was not present, somehow within the Space Saver's world it was easy for him to vividly envision her, tossing her long red hair and stepping serenely about, seemingly unaware of the beauty and charm she radiated. Not that Tim had a crush on her or anything. He was happily married and would never be unfaithful. Besides, Dora didn't take much notice of him.

Dora. The window flickered again. She turned and glanced at him with those astonishing ocean-blue eyes. Her image shimmered and faded, dissolving, for only the sheerest moment into—yes, Spots. Darn it!

Tim shook his head vigorously to toss off his illusions. There was no Smell. There were no Spots. In a sense, there was also no Dora, not for him.

There was only this claim, which he needed to finish. Or rather, to finish making a case for passing it on. He stifled a sigh and read on in a silent monotone with minimal comprehension.

Having reread all the documents, uselessly, he glanced up at the clock across the room. Its hands were still, like letters carved upon a gravestone.

Somehow, as always, the day crawled agonizingly by, and the time finally came for Tim to go home, after most of his co-workers had left, since he'd been a bit late. He removed his head from the terminal—as always, it emerged with a plop—blinked at the dinginess surrounding him, mopped his sweaty forehead, limbered up his legs and wobbled out of the office and down the flights of stairs. As always in the evenings, he took the bus. The horses were only for getting to work in the morning.

He was relieved but impatient as the crowded bus crawled along the street, following its tediously winding route through the heart of the city, stopping every block and a half to let other beleaguered downtown office workers on and off. Finally, it reached the first suburban outskirts, where Tim's home was located. He became rather giddy with anticipation as he stepped off the bus and grew nearly inflamed with pleasure as he rushed faster and faster, to the welcome mat which lay at the threshold of the castle within which he was king.

Once inside, he slammed the door, shutting out the world of work and other people. He felt his power kicking in. Like a turned-on air conditioner, it hummed with energy, bringing quick refreshment. Yes, here he was the person-in-charge, the boss, the director, even, and all his troubles at the office, even the unpleasantness that morning—which now seemed so long ago— evaporated from his mind. He dropped into his overstuffed recliner positioned directly before the TV set, stretched out his legs with a contented sigh, took up his remote from the lamp table beside him and savored the moment.

Ahhhh. This was what made it all worthwhile. Work could be difficult, but by comparison, his life at home was sheer bliss. Or so he told himself, setting aside his recent concerns.

Later that same evening, Tim sat contentedly in his recliner a couple hours past sunset but still some hours before his bedtime, licking up the last globs of a fudge bar from its wooden stick. All the pleasures of his home life surrounded him. On the end table at his side were his pipe stand and ashtray, as well as the remote for the TV set. The TV itself was satisfyingly large-screened and stately. Seated before it, quiet and obedient, were the twins, Clark and Shirley.

On the wall behind Tim's recliner was the steel-and-glass framed painting which had caught his attention that morning. It was a slick airbrush rendering of an elk posed serenely before a lime-green nuclear cooling tower, from the top of which a curving rainbow spouted out across a cloudless blue sky.

From the next room came the drone of a vacuum cleaner. Betty was busy as usual, keeping their home in its constant state of neat-as-a-pin-ness.

The vacuum didn't interfere with their TV viewing, for the set was still not turned on. The twins stared at the gray screen with blank expressions, looking a bit uncomfortable and stiff in their starchy playwear. Tim sucked on his pipe, humming to himself contentedly, along with the sound of the vacuum. He was still wearing his suit and tie from work—it was remarkable how comfortable his tie was—and he smiled softly, as though his moustache, which was now lying down properly, tickled the corners of his mouth in a most pleasant fashion. Thoughts of his particular troubles of as recent as, perhaps, that very morning, were far from his mind.

He decided to have another fudge bar. "Fudge bar, honey!" he called out to Betty. Then, at last, he remembered the TV.

"Well," he barked, slapping his knees, "we should turn on the old box and see what's on, shouldn't we?"

"Yes, Daddy," said the twins in unison.

Tim turned on the set with the remote to a loud electronic hum. He immediately began flipping through the channels.

"Daddy, can we watch—" cried Clark, but his father flipped past it.

"Hey, I'd like to—" said Shirley, but it was gone, along with the rest of her sentence.

"Ah, here's something good," said Tim.

The sound of circus music and applause came from the set. On the screen were three chimpanzees in yellow Easter dresses, riding tricycles in circles, while a brilliantly smiling girl in a spangled red corset and evening gloves, net stockings, high heels and a black top hat cocked to one side, holding aloft a whip, scampered after them, flinging her arms about. Except for the outfit and the smile, the girl looked rather like Dora from work.

The twins sighed quietly but didn't fidget.

"Isn't it amazing," said Tim, "the tricks they can teach those little creatures to perform?"

The sound of the vacuum grew louder as Betty pressed on toward the entrance to the living room.

"You can do that later, dear," said Tim without raising his voice, "and please don't forget my fudge bar."

The vacuum clicked, and its drone sighed quickly away. Tim pressed the up volume button on the remote. The chimps were now doing somersaults through hoops to loud applause, each receiving a treat from the top-hatted girl as they completed their task.

"They're regular little acrobats," observed Tim.

The twins made no reply, and their faces showed nothing.

Betty stepped into the room, carrying a fudge bar, Tim's third for the evening. "What are you watching?" she asked, glancing at the TV.

"Monkeys," said Clark and Shirley.

"I can see that."

Tim noticed Betty sounded just a bit irritable. He hoped she wasn't in one of her moods again, because he didn't really like to force her to behave. Well, sometimes he did enjoy it a little, in a way, but generally he'd rather not bother with it.

Betty stepped over to Tim's chair, handed him his fudge bar, then leaned close to speak into his ear.

"Did you take care of the bills?"

"Yes, I did, last night. Ulp, there it goes!"

A drumroll sounded from the TV, and the whip cracked as a chimp jumped feet first from a low diving board unto a trampoline, bouncing with a grimace and a shriek.

"All of them?" asked Betty pointedly.

"Of course, dear." Tim kept his eyes on the TV screen as he slurped at his treat.

"Then you did pay that Bliss Assurance thing again?"

This was a question Tim had anticipated.

"I paid all of the bills, Betty," he said with a certain finality.

Betty leaned back, folded her arms and spoke in a brisk tone. "Tim, I think we need to talk about this."

"May we be excused?" said the twins eagerly.

"May they, Tim?" said Betty, deferring to him.

"We have homework to do," urged Shirley, while Clark nodded.

"They have homework to do," Betty agreed.

"You may be excused to go do your homework," said Tim. The twins rose immediately and rushed up the staircase.

Betty stood and watched Tim watching TV while Tim glanced back at her sidewise and furtively. Her arms were folded, and her hair was disheveled. She looked rather tired.

"You know, Tim," she said finally, "you're always so content about things anymore. It doesn't take much to make you happy, does it? You just stay happy all the time now."

Tim cocked his head, as though he was considering this. "Well, reasonably so. I don't suppose there's anything wrong with being happy." He paused, fidgeting. "And life isn't all leisure, now is it? I do have to work, you know."

"But you always say that you like your job."

"Well, of course I do! It's a part of my job to like my job! But I work hard, and when I'm not at work, I think I have the right to enjoy myself a little."

Betty sat down on the edge of the recliner. "But don't you ever just get . . . bored?"

"Well, that's just silly, Betty," said Tim. He wished she wouldn't be so negative. "There's always something fun to do, say, something good on TV."

"Yes, you're right," she replied, interrupting him. "It's silly to waste time being bored. I was just thinking about that today." She sighed and furrowed her brow. "Tim, how long have we been paying that Bliss bill now?"

"Well, let's see," said Tim cautiously. "I don't quite remember. For some time, I think. I can't remember when we weren't paying it."

"Yes. Your memory isn't very good, is it? Anything unpleasant just seems to slip right out of your head." Betty's voice betrayed a trace of spite.

"That may be, dear," replied Tim. He could see that, as master of his household, he was going to have to put his foot down.

"And when it comes to this bill, we don't even know what it's for, do we?"

"That's just not so, Betty. It's for . . . it's . . . it's some kind of insurance policy. It's probably connected with work. I'll have to remember to ask someone about it."

"You already asked at work and no one knew about it, you said. More than once," insisted Betty. "Besides, the company is Bliss Assurance, not insurance, and the bill always says something about 'home coverage.'"

"I'm sure they offer home policies at work," said Tim. "I don't remember now who I asked. Maybe I should ask Personnel. But there's no reason to fuss over it, Betty."

"Tim, policies for what? I just cannot see sending money off every month to some company when you don't even know what you're paying for."

"Now, Betty," he said firmly, "you're being quite unrealistic. This company sends us these bills every month without fail. They expect us to pay them. They wouldn't be sending them if they weren't *for* something, now would they? Must we discuss this any further?" He looked directly at her, raising his eyebrows and exerting his authority.

Betty's eyes widened, refocused. As she spoke, her voice became softer and slower, its insistent tone draining away. "But why should we throw good money . . ."

At that, her mouth closed tightly.

"I'm ready for another fudge bar, dear," said Tim.

Betty stood abruptly and walked out of the room, heading for the kitchen.

"And while you're at it, honey," Tim called out contentedly, "get one for yourself, and for the kids! I'd like everyone to enjoy one! Oh kids! Come back down here! Fudge bars!"

As the twins descended, their footsteps, slow and steady,

OFFICE MUTANT

could be heard dimly beneath the loud sonic flashes from the TV
as Tim punched through the channels again, making them
dance.

2.

Tim wasn't late for work again until one Tuesday about a month later. In any case, he knew it hadn't been long enough to have obscured the notion, in the mind of his supervisor Mrs. Henderson, that he had an occasional tendency to be late, which amounted to a flaw in his work performance that needed to be addressed. His occasional tardiness and associated matters could be traced back further than he wished to contemplate. Even so, on that morning, his alarm clock, though loud and grating in its ever-bitter harangue, had failed for some minutes to motivate him into getting up out of bed—or rather, as it happened, off the floor on which he'd found himself when he finally popped open his eyes, posed awkwardly with his weight placed upon his fore-arms and the left side of his face, with his torso curved upward and his bared hairy shins flung balletically in the air.

He knew upon waking he'd been dreaming again, and vividly, but all he could remember now was the dream had involved running in fear from some menace and falling nearer and nearer its clutches as the bed's billowy white landscape first swallowed and then, disgustedly, regurgitated him. The nature of his pursuer, beyond its essential malice, had been gradually but thoroughly blanked-out from his mind as he'd determinedly yanked himself together, whipped off his nightshirt, gotten dressed, tumbled down the stairs and out the door, leaped into his harness and hurried off to his destination, whipping the reins so furiously his horses had whinnied in helpless protest as they galloped through the streets toward downtown.

Betty? She'd started to say something or other as Tim was streaking out the door, but he hadn't caught it.

When he arrived at work, he found the security staff had roped off the front lawn of the building, while some bodies that had been left on the lawn were removed. Infrequently, disgruntled or despairing claimants would leave the bodies of relatives, most often children, whose deaths they blamed on the difficulties that were sometimes involved in gaining assistance from departments of the Bureau. This sort of occurrence was a public relations problem the Bureau always wished to clear away quickly, so it would gain as little notice as possible.

The horses, despite Tim's fierce insistence, balked at approaching the building from closer than a block away, most likely because they detected the smell of the corpses on the lawn, though Tim didn't notice anything himself. My, how would the horses respond if they visited Tim's office and got a snootful of the Smell up there? But then again, he wasn't sure anyone besides himself could detect that at all, or whether it indeed really existed.

He rushed inside and up the flights of stairs because the elevators were still out of service. At last he reached his office, huffing, but was surprised no prominently posed backsides were to be seen within his co-workers' cubicles. Where was everybody? He wondered for a minute whether Daylight Savings Time might have started up again—or else ended, however that worked—so rather than late he was actually almost an hour early. This was a desperately hopeful thought. He looked at the clock on the wall, and it showed it was the time he'd thought it was, as did his watch; he was a few minutes late. But it occurred to Tim there'd been a problem at least once before when DST came or went, with getting the clocks' times changed. But then again, this wasn't a Monday, it was Tuesday, and didn't they always change the time on a Sunday in the small hours of the morning? But maybe everybody had overlooked that on Monday and word had only gotten out when they got home from work yesterday. Gosh, you'd think somebody would have called him if that had been the case. But then he might have inadvertently prevented the phone from ringing with his, umm, his authority at home and all.

Well, all of those possibilities, he decided, were pretty unlikely, really. But could it be one of those funny holidays, the obscure ones? He supposed so, though usually when there was a holiday coming up, everybody talked about it, longingly, for some days before.

He knew he was grasping at straws. But in any case, there was nothing for him to do but sit down and get to work. There'd surely be some explanation, and if he indeed was late, the sooner he got to work, the better.

As he neared the Space Saver, it seemed to be making an odd gurgling sound. Somewhat reluctantly, he touched it, and felt a definite rapid shudder. He wasn't sure what was going on but, being late for work anyway, he plastered down his hair with both hands, fell forward unto the desk and jabbed his head into the pink petals of his desk terminal's orifice.

The terminal hummed, and the video portion turned blue as it always did when Tim would first view it at the start of his workday, and the usual few notes of welcoming muzak began to play. But this time, instead of blooming into a view of the office with himself sitting up at his desk, the visual just stayed blue, and the notes played over and over. Somehow, it was stuck. It was turned on but wouldn't do anything. In fact, the icons hadn't come up at all, had they? There were only three, each a depiction of a cute cartoon monkey; one with hands over his eyes, representing the video function, another with hands over his ears for audio, and the third with hands over his mouth, for the microphone that allowed for vocal interaction. Usually, they flashed by so quickly you barely noticed them.

"Monkeys," he commanded. Nothing happened.

"Monkeys!" he repeated, more loudly. Still nothing but blue and the muzak, as if on a loop.

Darn it! If something was wrong with the terminal and it needed to be rebooted, he needed the monkeys to accomplish that, even. Maybe he'd missed some new instruction about changes in the system. Maybe it was bad for the system to have just one unit on this way when it was otherwise not being used. Maybe the gurgling meant something. Tim waited, hoping a correction would take place all by itself. Or maybe another employee would come in and know how to start the system correcty and it would then work for him as well.

Oddly enough, while the repeating flourish of muzak was slightly irritating, just looking at the blue screen had an oddly calming effect on Tim. It occurred to him that that in itself might be bad, and maybe he should turn it off before it lulled him to sleep or into some fugue state where he'd be caught by Mrs. Henderson, or wouldn't notice if the thing caught on fire, or his heartbeat and breathing would just slow down and he'd be brain-damaged or even die—but the soothingness took over so quickly these thoughts went right out of his head. He even found himself free-associating rather contentedly about the blueness of the screen.

The first blue thing that came to mind was that Blue Hole Tim had seen as a child, maybe about 20 years ago already, when his family went on some little vacation trip. There was a very deep hole in the ground somewhere out in farming country in a remote part of Ohio that was filled with water and had become a minor and perhaps rather dubious tourist attraction. The water in it was, on its surface, very blue, so it was known as The Blue Hole. Some claimed the hole was either bottomless, came out on the other side of the Earth in China or somewhere, or at least very, very deep, and was the reason it was so blue. Tim was very struck by it when they'd visited, unexpectedly so. He'd actually stepped closer and closer to it and, even without thinking about what he was doing, stepped under the safety cordon to get right up close and stare into it, entranced by the blueness. He was torn out of his reverie when his father grabbed his arm and jerked him back, asking whether he didn't have any sense. But Tim's father wasn't present to pull him back now; he'd have to do it himself. He reminded himself he was at work and tried to focus on his present predicament with the Space Saver not having started up correctly.

But the blueness drew him in again, this time by making him think of Dora's eyes. They were blue, but were they really a shade similar to this? Wasn't it too much of a bright, hard blue? But The Blue Hole couldn't really have been this shade of blue yet, in memory, it was the same. At the thought of Dora's eyes, the screen seemed to split into two and develop pupils looking right back into Tim's, warmly, invitingly . . . the muzak even seemed to become more pleasant, more soothing as if shimmering somehow . . .

Dora again! He couldn't let himself think about her. After all he was a happily married man.

All at once it was as though the channel had changed on a TV set—or like he'd been yanked abruptly out of a pleasant dream when he'd fallen asleep on the couch by a too-loud TV commercial. The audio boomed with a voice Tim dreaded: Mr Grovel's. The screen wavered, and a distorted image of Grovel's round and flabby face appeared, a too-small pair of blurry-lensed black horn-rims were twisted spread-eagle across it, sweat glistening on his forehead and nose and running in rivulets down his cheeks, as he nervously chewed his swollen lips.

"OK, is this the whole crew?" said Grovel, looking around but not, it seemed, seeing Tim right in front of him. "Is Renner here? OK, there you are, didn't see ya. What are you up to, trying to hide behind Nan, afraid I might call on you? Heh-heh! Where's old Woody, is he here today?"

"He went to the restroom," someone said.

"Again?" said Grovel. "Oh, OK, here he comes. Gotta try spacing out those restroom breaks a little more, Wood, we got a meeting going here, everybody needs to hear this. Where's that other guy, that Plunker? Plummer? Not here? Did he call in again?"

Oh my God, it was a staff meeting! Tim must have forgotten it was coming up.

"I'm right here," said Tim. "Mr. Grovel? Here. Present."

There was some murmuring from off-screen. "What do you mean, you're not sure? OK, whatever."

Gee, he can't hear me, thought Tim. But you could attend staff meetings through the Space Saver, couldn't you? The rest of the staff outside of Preverification couldn't do that, they were all really present in person, as bodies in the room with Grovel. But Tim was pretty certain he'd attended meetings in this way before. Or had those been Preverification-only meetings?

Actually, Tim considered if he was supposed to be at the meeting in person it might be a good thing Grovel couldn't hear him, he'd just get flustered and mad. But where is the rest of the Preverifications staff, he wondered. The screen just showed Grovel's big fat face, and when Tim swiveled his head around, instead of the room around him, he saw only a blue blur.

At that thought, as if in response to it, the picture in front of Tim pulled back, further and further, and Mr. Grovel's face became smaller as his full figure became visible. And then, pulling back more, Tim was able to see some of his co-workers surrounding him.

There was old Nan Sputner, his former boss from Cert Ink, seemingly sitting next to him, and off to the side near the front of the room was Dora, alluring as always, wearing a pretty blue dress today—but it was kind of too blue, almost electric blue—and Mr. Drivel, Ted Porshinsky, Woody Prober (who was still ambling around choosing a seat after returning from the men's room), Marjorie Sawyer, Willa Klotz, Cal Bilger with his hands shaking as usual at this time of the morning due to his drinking problem, and Ernie Pizler from Supplications, Mrs. Clutter from Initial Registry, Mr. Renner from Verification Reconsideration wearing his orange-ish toupee today rather than the pinkish one, though it was looking a bit more pink-orange than usual, the newish downstairs receptionist Carlene or Darlene, and that woman from Supps, the tall attractive blonde with an old-fashioned flip hair style, and a lot of others. The whole bunch of them, in fact, including the Preverifications staff; there was Ellen and, uh oh, Mrs. Henderson and, sitting next to her in the front row, Sue Frisky.

But wait—why hadn't he seen them in their cubicles when he came in? Something was definitely wrong. Why weren't they using the Space Saver? The vague dread he'd been feeling began to increase and gain definition.

Even though he was able to turn his head and look around him, Tim had a strong sense he wasn't really there. The colors were too distorted, and everything looked kind of grainy. Stranger still, Mr. Grovel looked kind of melted, somehow. There must have been something wrong with the transmission or whatever.

Grovel was talking on, so Tim stopped ruminating and listened. "OK, folks, the big news is we're going to have a renovation of our offices. Get some new carpeting and some other changes to go with it."

Sue stood up and applauded. Mrs. Henderson, Nan and several others joined in, though remaining seated, and then most of the others present, though some with obvious reluctance. Tim participated as well, though his own clapping seemed out of sync with the rest.

"Thank you very much," said Mr. Grovel. "It wasn't my idea, but I'll be glad to take credit for it if it all works out."

"Who did make the decision?" asked Mr. Prober, who often spoke frankly lately, perhaps because he was within a few months of retirement.

"I, I don't really know, or care, Woody," said Grovel. "Order comes down from the board of directors, that's what matters to me. I'm sure experts made the decision—"

Tim knew, as certainly his co-workers did as well, that Grovel was about to deliver his favorite joke but was thwarted when Mr. Prober broke in again. "But OI came up with the idea, right, and our esteemed board rubberstamped it, right?" he persisted. "So what's the shell game this time? 'Cause you know they've got something up their sleeve again."

"Well, Woody," sighed Grovel, "now that's just the rumor mill, you can't go by what the rumor mill says."

"Turned out to be right last time," said Prober.

"Well, maybe it did and maybe it didn't. You haven't heard the plan yet, have you, Prober? OK, so these experts have decided—by the way, you know what the definition of an expert is, right?"

Tim recited the joke in his head as Grovel delivered it: "X is the unknown factor, and a spurt is a drip under pressure."

Mr. Prober cleared his throat while Mr. Drivel leaped from his seat, gave a loud braying laugh and applauded fiercely, as if anticipating more fun. No one joined in with his applause, nor did anyone else laugh. Grovel gave Drivel a brief resentful glance.

"OK, some of you may have heard that one before. Anyway, our experts at Central Office have determined we need new carpeting, and it may be true the old one had some, somebody thought anyway it had some kind of whatever on it."

"It had mushrooms growing on it in Supplications! Remember that?" It was Nan talking this time, and the tall blonde turned in her seat to nod emphatically while several others murmured something that sounded like "Oh yes."

"OK, right," said Grovel, "somebody thought they saw some mushrooms or something on it, and a complaint was made and there was a big stink and they came out and fumigated the carpet or whatever, so if there ever had been mushrooms or whatever in the first place, they weren't there anymore. OK?"

"But it was badly stained, and you can still smell the insecticide all the way over in Registry," said Mrs. Clutter.

Hmm, thought Tim. Insecticide? No, it never smelled like that.

Tim noticed Sue Frisky holding up her hand to be called on, but Mr. Grovel apparently didn't notice or, perhaps, was ignoring her. The others were just speaking without being called on.

"Well, a mushroom is not an insect the last I heard, so I doubt they sprayed any insecticide. Anyway, who*ever* it was who made the anonymous complaint about mushrooms growing on the carpet, you have them to thank for this new project and all the disruption that goes with it. Now, the carpet we're getting is from another office—"

"So it isn't a *new* new carpet, Mr. Grovel?" asked Nan, pouting.

"Well, what I'm told by Central Office is it's a new carpet, but it was installed in another office that was subsequently never used."

"Oh, poo," said Nan.

"Was it a BV office?" asked someone else. "The one in Stankerton?"

Mr. Grovel sighed. "No, I understand it was at an office unrelated to the Bureau. Might have been out of the state or out of the country for all I know. In any case, the carpet is already cut to fit an office that is similar but not identical to our own, therefore, some changes will have to be made to accommodate the shape of the new carpet."

"That's backwards, Roger, isn't it?" said Mr. Prober, smirking. "What are they going to do, knock the walls out?" Prober looked over at Tim, and their eyes seemed to meet, though Prober made no sign of acknowledgement.

For a long, still moment, Tim felt his vision pull away from himself, and he was viewing Mr. Grovel from a somewhat different angle. Grovel looked strangely different, older, stupider somehow, kind of like a clown, but one who was only mildly amusing, and mainly contemptible.

Mr. Grovel scowled. It was well known he didn't like to be called by his first name by staff, despite his informality with them, and, Tim could tell, was getting fed up with all the questions. "I have no comment about that, OK, Wood? I will say, though, I understand the carpet is being cut where it's possible to do so, so it's not all going the same way. The new carpet which we'll be getting was presumably cheaper than an uncut carpet which had not been installed anywhere, but with the budget cuts we're probably lucky to get even a used new carpet, not that this one has actually been used."

Tim then looked over at Dora, somehow dollying in front of

her like a movie camera. He was alarmed to see her blouse open, her breasts exposed, with swollen and erect nipples. Embarrassed, he pulled away, felt something crackle, and found himself again viewing the scene from his own perspective. He didn't look back at Dora, however.

There was some murmuring, and someone began coughing hard. Sue Frisky raised her hand again and spoke without being called upon.

"Mr. Grovel, since next week we're to be introduced to the Perpetual Quality Improvement system via the upcoming workshop, and I've been reading up on the system in preparation, I wonder if we should anticipate applying the PQI method to the period of transition in which we'll be dealing with—"

With a sudden whistling sound and then an ear-splitting boom, a large object came crashing down from above and completely obliterated Sue, ending her statement in mid-sentence. It was, Tim could see after it stopped vibrating, a gigantic anvil. It seemed to be standing flat upon the floor with no trace of Sue's remains beneath it. None of the others at the meeting seemed to notice this strange event had taken place or even that Sue had suddenly shut up or, for that matter, had spoken at all.

Nan spoke again. "But how did they find this unused carpet, Mr. Grovel?"

"I understand a consultant was hired who searched around the world and found just the right carpet for us, almost. Any other questions about the carpet?" Grovel challenged.

"When will it be installed?" asked Carlene or Darlene.

"Thank you! Thank you for that practical question! The project has started today, even as we speak. The installers are already here, in fact. Some of you might have seen them in the hallways. They're taking measurements."

"In other words, they aren't installing it yet," said Mr. Prober.

"They're so little!" commented Carlene or Darlene.

"Well, I'll tell you. They are a foreign firm, which I assume made the low bid. It goes without saying, but I'd better say it anyway, there's to be no comments made to or within earshot of any of the installation staff about them being foreigners. They're not supposed to speak English but you never know."

There was a question Tim didn't make out because he was distracted by the thought that he'd seen little men with big heads scouting around the office a week or two ago, murmuring together in what seemed to be a foreign language. But weren't they gone already? He hadn't seen them again. Apparently, they were coming back.

"Where are they from? I heard they're from Bassarabia. That true?" asked Ernie Pizler.

There was more murmuring.

"I have no idea," said Grovel. "I have no idea where that is, sounds like Eastern Europe. You're Polish, Porshinsky, you know where that is? In Eastern Europe?"

Mr. Porshinsky shrugged. "Not sure where? Well, we're in the same boat, then."

"In southeastern Europe," said Ernie Pizler.

"There you go, then," said Grovel.

Nan asked, "What offices are going to be done first?"

"Did everybody hear that? Nan just asked what offices are going to be done first. That's a very good question, but I'm afraid, right now, I can't answer that. I tried to find out from Central Office, but no one is currently available who can offer

45

details of the project."

"What about the dwarves from, where is it?" asked Mr. Prober, not smiling this time.

"Bassarabia. I tried asking the representative that called, but they couldn't enlighten me because, as I said, apparently they do not speak English. By the way, we've been asked not to utter the word dwarves while they're around. Apparently this is the only word in English they know, and they take offense at it. They're sensitive. Everybody's sensitive now."

"So this is subcontracted, too," said Mr. Prober, shaking his head.

"You betcha," said Mr. Grovel. "I just said they probably made the low bid."

"Doesn't even the boss of the crew speak English?"

"It's not been made clear to me which one is the boss. I thought maybe the tallest one was, but that didn't work out, I don't think. Maybe there isn't a boss. Maybe Bassarabia used to be a Communist country, so they don't have bosses. Maybe it still is."

There was murmuring.

"Alright, let me clarify, the comment about Bassarabia being a Communist country, that was a joke, it does not need to be repeated, OK?"

Tim raised his hand to ask a question and kept his hand in the air for a few moments. It occurred to him, however, he didn't have a question to ask, so he lowered it again. Good grief, what was wrong with him today?

Now there was insistent murmuring, but Tim still couldn't make it out, though he was in the room. There was something wrong with the audio. Or was it with his ears? It must have been that. His eyes, too, because the color was starting to get weird, more garish then before. Mr. Grovel's face now seemed to be elongating.

"I can't answer that at this time. I'm trying to get clarification from our friends at Central Office on what the schedule is for whatever changes they are going to make." There were murmurs. "How will we know in the meantime? Well, we'll know when they start moving stuff in a section that that section is moving. I want to add, to emphasize, you must go through hierarchy to get information, that is, everyone here must go through me, or else we'll both, we'll all be in hot water. Is that understood, everybody on the same page here?"

All it once it struck Tim that Grovel hadn't called on him and the others couldn't see him—it was because he was a ghost, a phantom, a spirit. Dead! This notion struck Tim as so shocking he felt something within himself disintegrate and, for a moment, couldn't think at all, as if he had fainted internally, though he sensed he was sitting there as before. Then, immediately, in place of his ability to form thoughts arose another entity, one in great despair, whose thoughts he could perceive, alien as they were. The only thought produced by this alien presence was a wordless and desperate urge, to get up, to run like hell from the room and the building and to never, ever return.

At that moment, Mr. Drivel came careening with great agility down the aisle on a skateboard. No one seemed to notice him at all, but he winked, it seemed, directly at Tim. Zooming before the row of seated staff members that included the blond woman from Supps, he grabbed her up. Glancing her over admiringly, his smile widened and his teeth became fangs. His head sprang forward and back in an instant, cobra-like, ripping away her entire face as if he had unmasked her. She shrieked as blood gushed from the edges of her exposed skull and bulging eyeballs, soaking her hair and clothing as he zipped away on his board, his hand under her dress and clutching her parts hidden there. Grovel went on talking, with the full attention of his audience, except for Tim himself.

Tim was distracted by a loud knock, which seemed almost to hurt his head. When the knock came again, he struggled to pull his head out of the terminal. When he did, he saw Mrs. Lumpkin, the custodian, standing before him, leaning on her vacuum cleaner and watching him with a skeptical expression.

"What in the world you doin', Timmy? You listening to music in there?"

"Oh, excuse me!" said Tim. "Umm, hello, Mrs. Lumpkin. I was, I was just watching a staff meeting." With his head pulled out of the machine, the Smell was hitting him hard. It was like rubber burning but with a hint of overcooked sauerkraut.

"On that?" she asked, pointing to Tim's terminal "It ain't even working. It's renovating."

"But it must be on," said Tim. "Isn't it?"

"It's not s'posed to be, but it's hummin'. I swear, that thing just scares the daylights out of me sometimes."

"Well," said Tim.

"They havin' a staff meeting down the hall," said Mrs. Lumpkin. "That's where everybody is. Is that the one you watchin'?"

"Oh really, where? But I thought it was, it was a Space Saver meeting."

"It's just a regular meeting today, 'cause they changin' the setup again. You was probably s'posed to be there, weren't cha? Everybody else is there. It's about this damn project they got going, another one. Got everything all messed up. I can't even do my vacuuming. Can't get anything done anyway 'cause those little men keep gettin' in my way."

"You mean the dwarves?"

"Well, they little but I wouldn't say they dwarves." There was a slight tone of scolding in her voice. "I'd say they midgets."

"Isn't it about the carpeting they're installing?" The Smell was becoming so bothersome he was tempted to grab his nose but knew Mrs. Lumpkin would be offended. He wondered for a moment if it could be coming from her but dismissed the notion.

"New carpet? That's them dwarves, puttin' in the new carpet. These new ones just little. I don't think you should call 'em dwarves just 'cause they little."

Voices came from down the hall, at first muttering, then garbled and strange as they drew nearer. Tim looked up and was surprised to see a group of very short men enter the room. They were all dressed alike, in spanking new overalls and caps, and seemed too preoccupied with their conversation to take any notice of him. One of the little men took a measuring tape from his bulky pocket, and he and the others broke into a practiced formation, pulling the tape this way and that and speaking all at once. The language they spoke, Tim finally realized, was foreign. But they did not have big heads like dwarves.

They worked their way from one end of the room to the other, making measurements and chattering away like birds in the morning, while Tim sat watching them with a blank expression. They did not even glance back at him. If they had, Tim would certainly have looked away or pretended to be working again.

Then other voices came from the opposite end of the hall. These voices were both loud and familiar. There was laughter and a sense of rambunctiousness. The voices were those of his co-workers. On that side of the hall was the room where staff meetings were held. Tim began to get a sinking feeling.

"Timmy! There he is!"

It was Nan Sputner who spoke and, coming up behind her along with all the others, was Mrs. Henderson, who gave Tim a most disapproving look. Sue was beside her as usual, smirking and not looking crushed by an anvil at all. But the blonde whom Mr. Drivel had bitten and abducted wasn't among them.

"We missed you at the big meeting!" said Nan. "Were you out here?"

"Big meeting?" asked Tim in a voice that shriveled like styrofoam in fire. He didn't want to say he'd thought he was watching the meeting on the Space Saver when he wasn't sure it worked that way and wasn't even sure it had been on.

He watched as his co-workers came streaming down the hall fearful Mr. Grovel might be among them. Mr. Drivel came striding down the center. With his hands in fists and swaying his arms about, he sang in an affectedly deep voice, "Joshua fit the battle o' Jericho, an' the walls come tumblin' down!" Mr. Renner loping forward and straightening his toupee, now fully orange again, chuckled at Drivel's antics, which only made him sing louder.

"So, getting a brand new Space Saver, eh?" said Mr. Prober. "Gonna sell the old one for scrap metal?"

"I wish," said Grovel. "It's not going anywhere, just being upgraded."

"Well, saves space, I guess," said Mr. Prober. "Need more elbow room around here anyway. Long as I don't have to work with it."

"You're lucky, you'll be out of here in six months," said Mr. Grovel.

"Maybe sooner," said Mr. Prober, cheerfully.

"Well, whatever. I'm off to Central Office for some more fun-time over there." Mr. Grovel turned to leave.

"Cheers," said Mr. Prober, but Mr. Grovel didn't respond.

Nan tapped Tim on the shoulder. "Did you hear the news, Tim?" she said, smiling with all her teeth. "We're going to get reorganized and reoriented!"

"Re-?" said Tim.

"It's a project Central Office has been planning for some time. They're going to move offices around as part of the big Space Saver upgrade."

"Central Office, ha! You mean OI," said Mr. Prober. "They're running the show now."

"Oh," said Tim, concealing his lack of enthusiasm. "That's nice." He wanted to ask whether they'd be changing the actual office or the office as it appeared when you had your head stuck up your terminal, but he was afraid that might be a stupid question.

"Yes, isn't that something?" she smiled dazzlingly, the crow's feet about her eyes crinkling deeply. "I think we all get tired of looking at the same old walls in the same old places." There was a hint of sarcasm in her voice.

"They're going to move the walls?"

"Yes, to put in the new carpeting, though that may be delayed now," said Nan, making a pouty face.

Mrs. Henderson broke in. "How is it that you missed the meeting, Timothy? You received a memo about it like everyone else. It said specifically the meeting would be in room 603, and he'd like everyone to be there in person."

"Oh, then I must have it here somewhere," said Tim, looking through one of the piles of paper before him. Then he remembered the memo would likely have only existed within the Space Saver, unlike the files themselves. But he'd just watched the meeting in the Space Saver!

"I said it was a memo, Timothy, those are your files," said Mrs. Henderson with wearied patience. "The message from Mr. Grovel told all of us to come to work fifteen minutes early today so we could learn about our reorganization project before work on it began." She glanced over at the little men, who were still measuring busily and chattering on in their strange language while paying no attention whatsoever to the returned staff.

"I don't think I've ever heard of Bassarabia," said Tim, eager to change the subject.

"They're not from Bassarabia, they're from Stygia," said Nan. "The other crew was from Bassarabia."

"Oh, I thought it was just that place," said Tim.

"No no no, that's where the dwarves were from, the ones who were going to put in the carpeting." She had intoned the word 'dwarves' very softly. "But somebody else got our carpet, so they're going to find another one. Anyway, today they said this crew is from Stygia. Ernie says it's in Austria."

It at last occurred to Tim he must have listened to the wrong meeting! It was an old meeting he must have been watching a recording of. He didn't even know you could watch recordings in the Space Saver. Maybe. Why not? Do they even know what all it does?

"I'm sorry I missed this and the last meeting, Mrs. Henderson. But I was able to review the last meeting on the Space Saver."

Mrs. Henderson stared at him. "Timothy. You were at the last meeting. The one about the carpeting. Don't you remember?"

"Oh, yes," Tim said, in some confusion but with an eagerness to agree with his supervisor. "I mean, I forgot." He decided not to hazard trying to explain any further.

Mrs. Henderson shook her head and was about to speak again when Nan changed the subject.

"It's funny when they bring in contractors they're always, umm, you know . . ." Nan widened her eyes to express the significance of what she left unspoken.

"I'm sure they'll do a very professional job," said Mrs. Henderson, bringing that particular line of discussion to a close. "At the meeting, Timothy, Mr. Grovel explained all about the reorganization and reorientation plan. I'm just sorry this has to be explained a second time because you didn't bother to read the memo Mr. Grovel sent to all of us. I hope you'll not let that happen in the future."

"Oh, I can fill Tim in, Marion!" said Nan. "Wanna stop in at the staff lounge awhile, mister?" Nan grinned like an alligator and extended her arm in happy invitation.

Nan was almost always friendly toward Tim, but there was something about her manner this morning that made him a bit wary. Once they were in the staff lounge, she closed the door behind them, saying in a near-whisper, "I'm just going to pull this to, so that we can have a little privacy."

The lounge had a pop machine, coffee machine and snack machine. None of the snacks were appetizing at all, most of them varieties of baked chips. The coffee from the coffee machine was caffeinated brown water. The soda pop was OK, but Tim didn't drink pop at work because it tended to make him burp.

He and Nan sat down together at one of the tables.

"It's been such a long time since we've really been able to talk!" said Nan, smiling so widely it seemed her face might split. "I only hear about you these days from Marion, who always tells me how well you're doing!"

"Oh. Well, it's nice of her to say that," said Tim. Actually, it was hard for him to imagine Mrs. Henderson saying such a thing, but Nan always tried to be sunny.

"I know Marion can be caustic at times, but that's just her way. Her father was in the military, you know. He was a Major. As for us in Cert, golly, we're just so shorthanded. We don't have anybody who's a real fast worker and problem-solver like you always were. I was just telling Marion the other day how much we miss having you."

"I, umm . . . thank you." He didn't like the sound of this, dreaded what it might be leading up to. He did not miss Certification of Inquiries, where you had regular contact with new claimants who were already in rather desperate straits. He didn't sympathize with them so much as just not want to have to deal with them.

"I know you have big headaches in the Pre-vay section, too, my goodness yes, what with that horrible Space Saver thing and all. I don't think anybody's happy about it. Dora tells me Mr. Grovel won't go near the thing. Cert is smooth sailing compared to that and, of course, what with this new renovation, Pre-vay is only going to get worse."

"Well, it's strange, but we're getting by. I guess that's the wave of the future, so we may as well get used to it."

"Golly, that's not a future I want anything to do with! I know Marion would rather not have it there, though of course she's not the type to say anything. You know how loyal she is, even though leaning over that desk all day is just terrible for her back. That's why she tends to get a little crabby sometimes, really. And of course, she'll be retiring in another few years. Mr. Grovel was totally against it, but Central Office wouldn't budge. And you know, Woody is right that it's the OI company that's behind it, even though they're private and not really a part of the Bureau. They have a lot of government contracts, Woody says, with the Pentagon and all that. It's all some special program of theirs. Who knows what they're up to, using people as guinea pigs, same as they have with the claimants. Claimants can be a pain to work with, but I'm glad we do have claimant contact in Cert, because that way they can't put us in that thing."

"Sure," said Tim. He still preferred Preverification to Cert, precisely because he didn't have to deal with claimants there.

"Of course, Mr. Grovel's retiring pretty soon too. He can't wait to get out of here, and doesn't care who knows it."

"Yes, that's too bad." He wouldn't miss Mr. Grovel, who was a grouch, and rather paranoid about Central Office and everything associated with it, partly because of his Wee Nippy habit.

"The scuttlebutt is that Marion would be up for his job. I'm not sure she really wants it, but you know how she is, she'll take it if they ask, and I'm sure they will. Of course she'd be fine, but bless her heart, I don't think she'd be one to put up much of a fight with Central Office, and you really have to do that sometimes. Of course, if Marion becomes manager, the Pre-vay section head position opens up, and I expect Sue Frisky will get it,

because she's such a go-getter. Also, Marion would be in favor o
it, I'm sure."

"Really," said Tim. He hadn't heard this before and was appalled, though he kept his face guarded. "But what about Mr
Drivel? I mean, as office manager?"

Nan seemed to be guarding her expression now as well. "Oh
I think Ned is very satisfied with where he is. He's able to pursue
a lot of his own projects and doesn't really have anyone to answer to, here in this office anyway."

"But, I mean, he and Sue don't seem to, umm, see eye to eye
and I thought maybe . . ."

"That he'd keep her from becoming Pre-vay head? Oh no,
don't think he even cares at this point." Nan's eyes became a bi
hard. "Though I will say there can be a problem with Ned when
it comes to his attitude toward women. Above all, he should re
member the Bureau has a very serious policy about sexual harassment."

"He's harassed Sue?" Tim didn't mean to sound so incredulous.

"No, but she's noticed it in the case of other female employee:
and commented on it. The fact that some women are the type
who think it's OK doesn't make it OK." She scowled, unbecom
ingly. "Sometimes young men around here get the idea they're
big shots and have the run of the place and can get away with
whatever they like, but they just might find out it isn't so, Bust
er. Present company excluded, Timmy, you're always so polite to
everyone." She smiled, though not as readily as before, and
looked away.

"Thank you," said Tim uneasily. "Umm, anyway, when i
comes to Sue, couldn't she maybe go to work in Cert instead

looking forward to . . .?" He decided not to finish his sentence.

"Oh, no no no! She wouldn't want that at all. She'd have a conniption if they tried to transfer her to us. It would be a step down for her, and you know she's all ambitious. And frankly, I wouldn't want her there, I just don't think it's a good fit."

"Oh. By the way, ummm, what's the name of that woman in Supplications who's tall and has blond hair?"

"Who?"

"The tall attractive woman with blond hair that's in kind of like a flip hairstyle, I think they call it." He was a bit embarrassed to describe a woman as 'attractive' after their exchange on sexual harassment.

"Oh, you mean Cheryl, Cheryl Pippin? She was in Supps but then she transferred to the supply office. She doesn't work here anymore."

"Really? She was at the meeting today, wasn't she? I mean, the previous meeting?"

"Well, no," said Nan. "How could she be there if she doesn't work here anymore? Maybe there was someone else who looks like her, though I can't feature who. Say, mister, how would you know who was at the meetings, if you weren't there? Unless you were spying on us." She laughed and slapped at his hand.

Tim shrugged. "I'm probably just mistaken, I guess."

"Yes, probably. Anyway, whoever's the section head, it's going to be a rocky ride there in Pre-vay, what with all these changes coming up. I'm not sure I'd want to be there until things straighten out. There's this new release coming up of Space Saver two point oh, which Mr. Grovel tried to get them to wait on, since they're going to have the renovation at the same time, but OI said it absolutely had to go on schedule because the two projects are connected, and you know how they always get their way."

"Umm, two point oh? What's that about?"

"Oh my goodness, that's right! You missed the meeting, and I'm supposed to fill you in. But we have been getting memos about it. You do read the office memos, don't you?"

"Sure, of course."

"Then, are you sure you're getting all of them? Maybe you've been accidentally dropped from one of the lists. I think there's more than one list."

The thought of having been dropped from memo lists bothered him. "Well, no, I mean, I do get some. Maybe I just—"

"Anyway, first of all they're taking out all the walls on the 6th floor, supposedly because of the new carpeting, though they also say we won't be getting new carpeting for a while." She raised an eyebrow meaningfully. "Then there's going to be a whole new version of the Space Saver that's more advanced. And some people say the real reason they're taking out the walls is because all the departments except Cert and Registry are going to be on the 6th floor, and everybody but us is going to be hooked up to the Space Saver."

Tim was unhappy to hear this, too. "But, but they don't all even have terminals! How could that work?"

"Well, some people say with this new version, you won't have to stick your head in your terminal anymore." She winked and frowned.

"Really? Well, that will be nice."

"I'm not so sure, Timmy. That way you'll just be inside the machine all the time. It'll have control over what you see all the time you're at work. And maybe when you're not."

"But, how could it do that?"

"I don't know, but Ernie Pizler knows all about computers and whatnot, and he says that's what OI has been planning all along."

"I see."

"I myself don't trust those Japs," she said, lowering her voice. "I know you're not supposed to say that, but my dad fought in the Pacific, and he told me some of the awful things they did back then. Ever since we've been working with them, the Bureau's gotten so nosey about their own employees, you know? I don't like the way they try to get into people's heads, monitor everything about them and make them over. In my day an employer let you have your own mind and your own personal life, they just cared about what you did on work time."

Tim nodded, though he didn't have any opinion about all that. All he knew about OI was the letters stood for something like 'Otomeshon Intefeisu,' and they were based in Japan.

"Oh, but Tim, you know what?" She gasped, made her mouth into a nearly round 'o' and covered it with her fingers. "I'm so silly! I'm not sure you did get a message about that two point oh thing yet. I think that was on the QT and I wasn't supposed to say anything. Oh dear! You won't tell on me, will you?"

"Uh, no of course not, but I'm just concerned to hear about this. It sounds so—"

"You know, I'm just getting so forgetful, and I don't really have anyone I can rely on in my section to remind me of things, I guess I'm just getting old and scatter-brained."

"Oh no, don't be silly. I mean, not silly, but just, that's not so."

Nan patted his hand. "Oh, you're so sweet! I guess I really

just mentioned it because I would hate to see you get involved with some crazy experimental project OI has come up with. Besides, you know, we really could use you back at Cert and I just think it would be so much better for you, considering everything. I know you had some issues with claimant-contact, but I don't know that I'd want to stay in Pre-vay if I were you, with these scary new developments going on. And to be honest," here she leaned forward and spoke in a stage whisper, "I know I have enough sway with Mr. Grovel to get you out of there, Timmy! I won't do it if you don't want to, but you really should give it some thought. Very seriously, Timmy. I worry about you up there." She touched his hand. "I hope you don't think I'm a silly old busybody, but we spend so much of our lives here at work, and I do care about the people I work with, and especially, well, especially some people that I like. You know?" She made another split-faced smile.

At that point, before Tim could reply, the lounge door opened and Sue Frisky came in.

"Oh, hello, Sue!" said Nan brightly. "I was just filling in Timmy here about our meeting, since he missed it."

Sue glanced dismissively at Tim. "Yes, Marion was wondering where he was."

Tim noticed that the Smell had gotten much worse just as soon as she stepped in. In fact, he'd almost forgotten about it beforehand. Maybe it was her.

Sue said, "So what do you think of our renovation project?"

"I think it's a very exciting time for Preverification and the entire Bureau," Tim replied.

"It certainly is that!" Nan hazarded another wink at Tim. "And next we have that improvement workshop, what is it called again? PDQ or something."

"PQI, for Perpetual Quality Improvement," Sue said. "I've read a great deal about it. It's one of the most advanced programs of its kind in the country."

Tim didn't know much about this, but wasn't really pleased to hear they were going to put the staff through another workshop program. He hated to be negative but, in his experience, such programs tended not to be terribly helpful and could be rather a trial. Come to think of it, Sue had mentioned this PQI in the meeting, just before the anvil crushed her. Gosh, maybe he wasn't getting memos, though it was true that he often just glanced them over.

"So, there's going to be how many workshops this time?" asked Nan.

Sue said, "I think it's a series of twelve workshops over six weeks. That's just the first stage. Of course, we'll be having the introduction session first of all, and that's Thursday for most of us."

"Are you scheduled for that one, Tim?" Nan asked.

Before he could answer, Sue said, "Yes, he's supposed to be here."

"It's all about administrators communicating better with employees, isn't it?" Nan said, "So they know what issues there are according to the people who do the real hands-on work."

"Yes, it's about how staff need to understand about paradigm shifts, that they can't just hang on to old ways of doing things when big changes in organization take place and they're still stuck in an old stale paradigm—"

At that point two more employees, a pair of young women from Registry whom Tim didn't know well, came in and sat at a nearby table together and immediately began to talk in rapid cheery voices, apparently about something that had been on TV the evening before. Sue sat down with them and leaned forward, eager to break in. Nan shrugged and smiled at Tim.

"Well, anyway, Timmy, keep in mind what I told you, OK? And when am I ever going to get to see that girl Betty again? And those two little boys of yours, how old are they getting now?"

"They're seven. No, eight . . ."

He was just about to add that one was a girl, when Nan glanced at her watch and said, "Oh my goodness, I have to run! Bye-bye, talk to you later!" She turned her head and said, "Bye-bye, Sue!"

Tim jumped up and went out the door right after Nan. Past it, she turned and smiled at him once again before rushing away.

The rest of the day crawled by with agonizing slowness. Though it had been an exhausting day and the Smell had at times been horrendous, Tim was too troubled on his bus ride home by what he'd learned in his chat with Nan to feel much relieved. Sitting there on the crowded bus, wedged in next to a fat woman and ignoring frail elderly people and small children standing up in the aisle next to him, he fretted. Nan trying to drag him back into Cert Ink was bad enough, but that he'd expected. The part about Sue Frisky possibly becoming the next head of Preverifications was a truly miserable surprise. Maybe Nan had just said that because she wanted to trick him into going back to Cert.

Yet what bothered Tim most of all, oddly enough, was his experience of 'attending' a staff meeting from some time ago through the Space Saver, and when it wasn't even turned on

The Space Saver was all about that, providing a benign field of illusion conducive to workplace efficiency, and it might have just been a glitch that it sent him to the wrong meeting; the old one must have been a recording. But as for it being turned off . . . could it have something to do with this new version of Space Saver Nanny told him about? How could it possibly leave something in your head that made it as though you were inside it all the time?

He was so preoccupied with his fretting he almost missed his stop and drew stares when he leapt up and threw himself out the door, stumbling a short ways down the sidewalk before catching his footing.

As he turned his usual corner and approached his home he noticed Betty leaning out of the bedroom window upstairs, watching the street with an anxious expression. She must have seen him just as he saw her for she pulled her head back and, a few moments later, he heard heavy footsteps coming down the stairway inside. Just before he could grasp the doorknob, Betty threw open the door, eyes hard upon him and wearing a grimace.

"Timothy," she said, "we need to talk."

"Why, Betty," said Tim, interrupting her, "how nice of you to be waiting for me at the door after my long, difficult day at work." He noticed her hair was quite an unkempt mess, as though she'd just gotten up, though it was rather late in the afternoon. And had she always had those odd lime-green highlights? Perhaps the light was funny or he was still a bit woozy from his experiences earlier in the day. "Where are the twins?"

"They're in the bathtub. Quit gawking at me and look at this, Timothy. Bliss wants twice as much money now!" She thrust an unfolded piece of paper into his face. It was stamped in large red letters 'Special Notice.'

"Now, Betty," he said, "you know that it's my job to open the mail. Your job is to take the mail from the mailbox and leave it for me on the coffee table."

"But look at it, Tim!"

"I will, dear, but really, let me step into the house first." He elbowed past Betty, disturbed at her odd behavior. He sat down at the living room couch, the proper place for reading the mail, though he really preferred not to look at it the very minute he came in the door.

"Alright, let's see. So it says—What? Why, this says they didn't receive my last payment!" The paper rattled slightly as Tim's hand shook.

"I know what it says!" said Betty.

"But I put the payment in the mail, I'm certain I did! And. . ." The paper rattled, a bit more loudly. "They say they're giving me a deadline for payment or they'll terminate services!"

"The nerve of those people!" cried Betty, brandishing her delicate fists before her.

Tim shook himself all over like a wet dog, became still, and set his jaw. "Well. There must be some mistake. I'll take care of it immediately."

"Then you'll call and tell them off?" said Betty, eyes flashing.

"No, of course not. I must not have sent the payment after all, or they wouldn't have sent this Special Notice. I'll write them a check right now. Be sure and give the letter to the mailman tomorrow so we know that it's been taken care of."

"Tim," screeched Betty, "how can you *do* that?"

"Well, it's simply necessary, Betty. You've seen the notice yourself."

Tim avoided giving more than a glance to the elaborate expression on Betty's face, rose from the couch and stepped awkwardly past to his recliner, in which he sat down, rather pointedly. The chair didn't seem as comfortable as usual, but the remote was on the end table, and he lifted it and punched the TV to life. It erupted with a scream, which for a moment he thought had come from Betty, but in fact, he had happened to start up the set on a passionate moment in a late afternoon soap opera. A moment later, he heard Betty in the kitchen, apparently washing dishes. She was banging the pots and pans rather loudly as she did so.

He shut his eyes and furrowed his brow as he tried to put the unpleasant situation from his mind. He was at home, after all. Problems were only supposed to be at work.

Gradually, Tim's body relaxed, molding itself into the recliner. Eyes still closed, he called out to Betty in as soothing a voice as he could manage.

"Betty? What's for dinner, dear?"

There was a long silence, and Tim opened his eyes with dread. Betty stood before him, blocking the TV, glaring at him. "You are simply throwing away money when you pay that bill which you've already paid and which you don't even know what is for in the first place."

"Betty," said Tim, drawing up his authority as head of the household, "please don't block my view of the television, and answer my question."

Betty stood there motionlessly, her nails dug into her palms, mouth set into a narrow line, devils dancing with rage in her eyes. Tim looked back at her, mildly but steadily.

After some moments, Betty began to tremble. The trembling

worsened until it seemed she must fall over or spring on top of him. But instead, with a long, caterwauling yelp, she ran from the living room and into the kitchen.

Betty's yelp, though garbled, was intelligible to Tim. Though still fretful over his problems at work, Tim was rather pleased to learn they would be having meat loaf and mashed potatoes.

3.

Tim went to work. The horses seemed tired and clopped along slowly, though traffic was rather light.

The elevators were all working—at least, none bore out-of-service signs. He didn't see many claimants and no obviously angry ones at all, just a few sitting quietly by themselves and wearing woebegone expressions. He boarded an elevator no one was in except himself. It rumbled upward.

Things seemed to be going well until the elevator door opened. It looked like he was on the wrong floor, but the elevator's digital banner above the door showed otherwise.

Tall, slender workmen whose eyes all seemed to be oddly close together were dragging huge beams of wood around, like busy Jesuses calmly following stations of the cross, and setting them up in a row against the wall. There was talking, muttering and shouting, but no words registered in Tim's mind and, indeed, none were addressed to him. He was distracted by the sight of the backdrop for the workmen's activity: the corridor was much narrower than before, and the entrances to the connecting corridors were, simply, gone. Thus, there was a single narrow corridor.

Tim went down it, trying to stay out of the busy workmen's way, but after walking a long ways, he did not come to any connecting entrance. He started back the other way and was approaching the elevator—oddly, there was only one, though there'd been a bank of six elevators on the ground floor—when he heard Mr. Drivel's voice.

"Hey Timmy! What'cha doin' down there? Look like you're lost!"

Tim looked up. Drivel grinned down upon him from a trapdoor in the ceiling. His head, in fact, was turned straight down and hanging out of the trapdoor, as though he were suspended by his feet. He looked as happy as a small child on an amusement park ride.

"Um, gosh, I guess I don't know where—"

"Actually, you know, you can't get to your office on the sixth floor this way anymore."

"Oh, I didn't know that." Tim worried suddenly he may have missed yet another memo on this.

"You have to go to seven, and then walk down to six by the stairs."

"Oh. Alright, thank you." He rushed off toward the elevator feeling some trepidation about going to floor seven, as he'd never been there before.

"Hey Timmy, where you going?" called Drivel.

Tim turned and hurried back, narrowly dodging a pair of workmen carrying what looked like a very large, strangely over-inflated tuba, which judging from their postures and expressions was terribly heavy. "I'm sorry," he began.

"Aw, don't be sorry, Timmy! But you can't use that elevator to get to seven. They'll let you off on the wrong part of seven, anyway. You have to take the back elevators. Either start from the ground floor in the back elevators or go to three in the front elevator and go to the back."

"Oh." It occurred to Tim he didn't know how to get to the back elevators on three. He'd better go back to the ground floor, but didn't wish to say so, because Mr. Drivel might think he should know how to get to the back elevators on three. "All right, thanks," he said, and started off toward the elevator again.

"Hey Timmy, wait. You're not thinking of going to the ground floor, are you? Because you can't take that elevator back down to the ground floor. It'll only go down to three. It's a new security arrangement or some damn thing. Either that or yet another boneheaded mistake around here. It goes go all the way up, but not all the way down. See?"

"Oh. Gosh. So, how do I . . .?"

"Well, I could just pull you up. Here!" Mr. Drivel, grinning with all his teeth and much of his gums, grabbed Tim's hand and, with incredible strength and ease, yanked him through the trapdoor and, after a brief, head-spinning whirl, set him on his feet.

Tim stood, dazed, still grasping Drivel's hand.

"Just because I let you hold my hand on the first date, don't think you can try any funny stuff, you masher!" Laughing with satisfaction, Drivel pointed down the hall and said, "C'mon, let's join the gang!" and set off at an enthusiastic trot.

Tim hurried after him, fearing to be left behind in this unfamiliar environment.

Mr. Drivel ran so fast Tim couldn't possibly keep up. At the end of the corridor was a bright light, which Drivel literally dived into as he neared it, his image seeming to dissolve within it. Tim came after, warily.

Beyond the corridor, he was blinded by the light and fell to the ground that felt, strangely enough, like sand. A yellow spot hung far up in the sky over what appeared to be a sandy expanse, radiating heat—the sun But what was it doing inside the Bureau building? And what was that motion in the air that seemed to feel like a sea breeze? Were they, somehow, out by the seashore? But Ohio wasn't anywhere near . . .

At that thought, a colossal ocean wave emerged from the mouth of the sun and swept straight down at Tim, engulfing him. A moment later Tim found himself floating in a silver sea with a toy inner tube with a happy sea monster's head at its front stuck around his middle. Several beautiful girls, topless and with tousled blond hair, splashing water with mermaid tails and giving off an enticing fishy aroma, surged toward him and embraced him fondly.

They carried him off, finally tossing him with a happy shriek unto an island with a single palm tree, on which they immediately appeared again, having now sprouted lovely bare legs and wearing grass skirts with garlands of flowers around their necks, hula-dancing. Then, giggling, they grabbed Tim up and, carrying him like a surfboard, ran with him, the island expanding before them as a road, which soon went uphill. Tim craned his neck, trying to find where Drivel had gone, but they were nowhere in sight.

Just then, the sun grew very bright overhead. Looking up, squinting, Tim saw that the sun had become a round, yellow, happy-faced emoji. Breaking into a loud, goofy laugh, its mouth in so wide a smile its dimples jutted out from either side of its round face. It fell from the sky with a long, descending whoop, and the girls, now in skimpy bikinis of various bright colors, caught it and began to bat it back and forth like a beach ball. One of them punted it to Tim, calling "Look alive!" and as the sun came toward him, it shouted, "Cowabunga! Let's see what's over the bend! Follow the yellow brick road!" The sun's voice sounded oddly like Mr. Drivel's.

The road ahead, indeed, was bright and yellow as well, though no city could be glimpsed at the horizon. In fact, Tim could see nothing but haze. He pushed the ball, the girls running behind and yelling encouragement, but found that, after some minutes, he was getting badly winded. He wished some of them might help him push the tee-heeing sunball but didn't want to ask. He pushed the ball higher and higher, until he found he'd reached a pinnacle, beyond which was a steep descent, and the ball rolled down speedily as he stumbled down the hill after it. Finding himself at the bottom, he heard the girls calling to him from the top. "Come back up! C'mon, come back!"

Tim picked himself up, rolled the ball up the steep side, only to see the girls disappear just as he reached the top. He saw the ball, the former sun, was now gray, lumpy and hard, like a huge stone. He pushed it and found, to his alarm, his hands stuck to the surface of the juggernaut so that he tumbled down the side of the hill along with it, being rolled over by it repeatedly as they went. At the bottom, he was dazed, but looking up, he saw the girls again at the top, smiling and waving, urging him to push the stone back up again. He did so and rolled back down, repeating the act senselessly more times than he could count, as though compelled to by an impulse he could neither resist nor understand.

Tim couldn't have said how long this went on, but eventually he crawled away from the stone in exhaustion, twitching. The stone rose into the air, doubled and doubled again, became round and flat, and filled the sky above him as flat, yellow, blue and red Spots which, at a click like the flick of a light switch, went out.

The girls, giggling happily, rolled him over and stood about him, leaning forward and grinning widely. The breasts of an especially well-endowed one bobbed in his face. At the demand of another strange impulse, he opened his mouth more widely than he would have thought possible, took one entire breast in his mouth and easily bit it off. The girl fell backward and wailed as he chewed and swallowed, a little too quickly, as it hurt his throat on the way going down. It did, indeed, taste like fish. The girls scattered, screaming, except for the one who'd lost her breast, who was now collapsed into the sand, while one other girl bent over her, weeping frantically. Now ravenously hungry and enticed by the second girl's shapely buttocks, he sank his teeth into the one on the left, removing it easily. This time he chewed more thoroughly before swallowing and going on to the right buttock as the girl thrashed on the sand, shrieking at first, then muttering until she fell silent.

The two girls were both now fallen, bleeding, their eyes glassy and mouths ajar. The rest had vanished. He lifted one of the corpses, rapidly stripping its skeleton of flesh with his teeth. It was so delicious he ate half of the other corpse as well. Finish-

ng up, Tim felt strangely satisfied, perhaps more so than ever
before in his life. He fell unto his back in the bloodied sand and
passed out.

The next he knew, Mr. Drivel was standing over him in baggy swim trunks. "Hey, I'm sorry, I got distracted and kind of
forgot about you. Jesus, check out the carnage! Two of 'em, eh?
Holy Toledo, you're an overachiever." Drivel helped Tim get
up and dusted him off.

It was night, and they were out on a city street, near a street-
lamp. Tim didn't know how they'd gotten to this place from the
seaside. Oddly, his clothes weren't wet from his travail, perhaps,
he thought vaguely, because the sun had been hot enough to dry
them. "You look pretty beat, Tim. What say you and me get a
drink. We have a few things to talk over."

With his arm over Tim's shoulder, Drivel led him down an
alleyway to a small building with a flashing neon sign outside
that read YUM-YUMS and repeatedly depicted the outline of a
dancing girl, apparently unclothed, jumping through three different poses, in three different colors of neon.

"Wha . . . where are we?"

Drivel laughed. "We're where the girls are, where else? I
think Renner's in here too." Loud, throbbing music blasted out
abruptly when the door opened. Renner was sitting at a table,
gazing with open-mouthed glee at a nude girl standing on it and
flailing around a pole.

There was a bowl of toothpicks on the table, beside a bottle of
ketchup and another of steak sauce. Drivel grabbed a toothpick
out and handed it to Tim. "Here ya go, need one of these?" He
laughed heartily. "Too late for the ketchup."

"No thanks," said Tim, provoking more laughter from Drivel.

"OK, enough fun. We need to discuss a couple different things, Tim. First of all, you need to get with the program. You haven't yet got the hang of how to move around in the Saver System. You gotta make sure certain other people around here share your experiences of things when it counts, and that they don't at other times. You can't just let it be solipsistic. You know what solipsistic means, right?"

"Certainly." He made a note to look up the word later.

"It's like with missing meetings. It's OK to do, but you gotta put yourself in the meeting for others to see, even though you're not there."

"I know, I don't know how that happened, I just . . . I'm sorry, what did you say?"

"No no no, you don't get me. You put yourself in the meetings, but you don't attend. See, there's all kinds of stuff you could be doing with the system that you're not doing. But I can see you've got the potential. It's like when you dropped that big anvil on Frisky. That was a hoot, and you handled it very well. You've got a real natural ability."

"But . . . I didn't . . . that was a recording of a real meeting, wasn't it?"

Drivel laughed. "No, it was not a recording. It was last week, but you were there. Time and space, basically different aspects of the same shit. Raw material to work with, is how I think of it. So, like, you altered the meeting, in that you watched it in a different time stream and did one funny intervention that nobody else saw, but that's not enough, see? There's just all kinds of shit you could be doing. You know how it is at home, right, with your wife and kids? You exert your will and they do what you say, right?"

"Yes, but how did you—"

"Never mind. You could be doing that same shit at work, and more. Like, you could go back and alter that other meeting too, but we have more important things to concern ourselves with at this point." He picked up a salt shaker, poured a small pile of salt into the palm of his hand and licked it off.

"The other thing we need to discuss, Tim, is the opening in Cert."

A waitress, dressed only in a frilly apron and cap, served them large iced drinks with lemon wedges stuck in the top of the glass. Tim took a drink and coughed, perhaps at the drink, or at the reference to Cert.

"I already spoke to Nan about it a week ago," said Tim. "I'm really not interested, umm, at this time, because, I think working in Preverifications is really quite fulfilling, and umm, a challenge, and I look forward to the forthcoming challenges . . ."

Drivel slapped him on the shoulder and laughed. "C'mon, Tim, this is your ol' buddy Ned Drivel, you don't have to bullshit me! You don't even remember that, do you? That we used to hang out."

"Well, sure, you mean at, umm . . ." Actually, Tim had no idea what he could be talking about, unless it was the year they were both on the Social Committee, before it was cancelled for lack of interest.

"Never mind, Tim. The thing is, I'm not talking about some shit job in Cert, I mean department head. See, Nan doesn't know it, but she's on the way out, and I mean, soon. We're expanding the Saver system into the other departments, including Cert, and the old girl's just not up for it. We need someone with some experience working with the new system."

"Including Cert? But, but how can that possibly work? They have claimant contact!"

"Don't worry, the OI team has it all worked out. They're crafty, those Nips. Inscrutable, but crafty. Claimants are the same as files, anyway. Maybe a little more complex, but still, just bundles of information waiting to be fucked with."

"But there are other people who have more experience than me. Say, Sue Frisky, or—"

Drivel laughed. "Frisky I'm going to 86 as soon as I'm done toying with her." He shook his head. "Sue Frisky, Jesus. Talk about an icebox. Has a jaw like a dinosaur, too. Nope, none for me, pal. I don't mind a little kink now and then, but a masochist I'm not. Besides, I'm not talking about just the Saver itself, but Bliss."

"Bliss?"

"The Bliss program you're signed up with. The two are connected. You knew that, right?"

"Uh . . . oh yes, I did." So, the assurance plan had indeed come through his employer! He'd forgotten. He might mention that to Betty if she should complain about the bill again. But just then, he had to wiggle out of this Certification of Inquiries thing.

"Well, like I say you know how, with the Bliss policy, you can control the folks at home, the little women and the offspring? I need you to unlock that potential you have and start doing a little of that here at work, too. I can't handle the whole shebang myself, not for starters anyway. I need a man I can count on, who has the touch, can learn, and doesn't freak out over the pop-ups."

"Pop-ups?"

"You know, the stuff that pops up. The funny stuff. The not-normal stuff. You're used to it by now, right?"

"Well, I guess I am." Tim wasn't sure what Drivel was talking about.

"Actually, that little sequence with the ladies back there? That was actually kind of a test. And I'm glad to say, you passed with flying colors. You've really got the hang of going with the flow, bucko."

"Those girls," asked Tim cautiously, "were they employees?"

"Oh no, no. Anything like that we subcontract. But we get some pretty tasty tail that way. You agree, doncha?"

"I guess. I mean, yes."

"See, it's part of the deal with the Saver, if you've got the hang of it like I do, and like you're getting to have. But you've gotta keep out of my way, because I'm number one. That's just how it is. I get first call on the scarf nookie."

"But, I'm sorry if this is a silly question, but, why are we eating girls?"

"Well, partly because they taste good, but mostly just to gain satisfaction. You know, in a workplace like ours, you have to take a lot of shit off people, bitches especially. So it's a way to burn off those everyday frustrations. Hell, even I still have them. Plus I got a shitload of old grievances, believe you me."

Tim had another thought. "Do you ever, say, get rid of people you don't like that way?"

"People I don't like. Hmmm. Like who?"

"Well, like Sue Frisky."

"Sue Frisky?!" He laughed heartily. "Be my guest, sailor. Talk about barf city."

"So eating . . . women, is like . . ."

"We all have our kinks," smiled Drivel. "You too, I notice. The best part about it is, if you've got the balls to do it in the first place, you can really get your rocks off in an awfully satisfying way. Makes a big difference in your outlook on things. And outlook is damned important in an organization like ours. Given what I've seen today, I think you're ready to become not just the head of Cert, but a full Administrator 1."

An Administrator 1! Tim had never even aspired to reach that high. "But, I'm not sure Mr. Grovel will approve. He doesn't really have that high an opinion of me, I'm afraid."

"Grovel's on his way out, too. He doesn't even know, or want to know. Central Office doesn't even bother with him anymore. They know he spends half the day down at The Wee Nippy getting soused. Doesn't matter, he's effectively kicked upstairs."

"Oh." Tim glanced up to see that the dancer on their table, whom he'd barely noticed, was bending over in his face and tapping her finger playfully on her g-spot. Drivel looked up too, smiled and applauded. Renner made a mewling sound.

"But mister, I mean, Ned . . ." Tim hesitated. "This whole Bliss thing. How does it . . ."

"How does it work? Lucid dreaming plus telepathic projection. Your terminal at work charges you up for it. Plus there's a template that sets your basic attitudes. That's all."

"I see."

"Yeah, me too," said Drivel, laughing. "Anyhow, Tim. I know you had a little trouble here at the Bureau a while back, but they've got you all adjusted now, and the way that works, your rating is pretty much triple A around here. Well, double A, anyway. Whatever. *Fuckin' A!*" He hooted merrily.

Tim had a bad feeling about the "little trouble" comment,

which seemed to stir something within him, as if he was trying to reach something in a dream; but in a moment, the feeling had faded.

"You won't have to deal with the scuzzy claimants like Nan does, it's not going to be that way anymore. As for the staff, we can feed them whatever shit we like and tell them it's sushi. And it will be sushi! See? That's the beauty of it!

"You've paid your dues as a flunky long enough. I know that's not the real you. As for the template, you can break out of that cage. You've already started to, even if you don't know it. Time to jump over onto the other side of the fence, where you're serving up the sushi to the lower orders rather than eating it. Like me!" Drivel chuckled. "Well, not quite like me, but a hell of a lot better than you're doing."

"So, this is what you did for Mr. Renner . . ."

Renner was still watching the dancer intently and was now literally panting with his tongue hanging a surprisingly long way out of his mouth.

"Oh, is that what's worrying you? That's a whole different deal. Forget about it, you're not going to end up like Renner. I don't need another man's best friend." At that, he clapped his hands together and his laughter became unpleasantly high-pitched. "Anyway, there's the whole ball of wax, kiddo. Just wanted to give you the good news. It's a hell of an opportunity I'm handing you, hope you appreciate it. You do, right?"

"Oh, I, I do, Mr. Drivel, I really do," said Tim, though he still had some very grave doubts.

"Sure you do," said Drivel, clapping Tim hard on the back. "Well, toodle-ooo, pardner. Workshop tomorrow, you know."

Tim had, in fact, entirely lost track of time. He glanced at his watch, whose hands seemed to point scoldingly at an unbelievably late hour. "Oh my gosh, that can't be right! My watch must have stopped this afternoon!"

"Let's see," said Drivel, grabbing Tim's wrist. "Nope, 'fraid not, old sport. Sound as a dollar."

At that, Drivel rose out of his chair, grabbed the girl off the table and, carrying her like a sack of potatoes, headed for one of the doors in the back of the club. "Midnight snack," he said, turning his head and grinning at Tim. Renner, grinning at Tim as well, jumped down and frolicked after Drivel on all fours.

Tim had a lot on his mind when he arrived home, having walked since the buses were no longer running. He noticed as he approached his house there were several cars parked outside and a light was on in the bedroom upstairs. He keyed open the door and stepped inside and immediately heard a sound that froze him in place: a woman's shriek, from upstairs. It was Betty.

A moment later she laughed, happily and loudly, as if she could barely contain herself. It was a sound he hadn't heard in some time.

More puzzled than frightened, he took a step, then heard another laugh, interrupted by a moan, and then a quick succession of gasps. He was stalking toward the staircase when he heard a nearby voice.

"Hey, Tim."

Tim turned violently. Before him was the portly figure of Les Puller, from his bowling team. Les was an insurance salesman. He was standing in front of the open refrigerator.

"So you don't keep any beer in here, huh?"

"Uh, no. I'm, uh, sorry."

"You don't like to have a cold beer in the evening after a hard day's work? Boy, I do. It's my constitutional, like."

"What—just why is it that, um—is there some occasion?" It seemed impolite to ask outright what Les was doing in his house, and in his refrigerator. Beyond that, wondered Tim, what was—

He heard another shriek from the bedroom, followed by a long exclamation he could not make out. It was definitely Betty.

"I must say, the little woman is quite a girl, Timbo," said Les, clapping him on the shoulder. "Sorry about the penalty, but that's the deal, pally, three strikes you're out. Puttin' out, that is. Ha!"

Les took a seat in an armchair, one of Tim's chocolate sodas in hand.

"But what is—what are you . . ."

"Sit down, Tim, you make me nervous standing there like that. Hey, here comes the big man."

There was the sound of someone stepping downstairs, heavy steps. It was, Tim saw, another member of the team, Bill Duffy, who had some sort of construction foreman job. Bill was putting his shirt on, hand buttoning up from the bottom, removing from sight his hairy and muscular chest. "Yo, Tim." He then made a low, sharp whistling sound at Les. "So you don't like to watch, huh, Les? Gus Owens was up there watching like it's a football game. 'Course, now he's taking his turn, and you know Gus. Strictly a backdoor man."

"Ehh, that guy's sick. Got no sensitivity."

A long wail came from upstairs. There was a sound of bedsprings squeaking hard in a regular rhythm.

Bill said, "I don't really wanna watch either. I'd rather do it than look at it. Heh, heh!" Turning to Tim, who was now seated on the sofa with his hands clasped, he said, "So Tim, what's tricks? Where you been, bro? I thought sure you'd show up to-night, what with the de-fault an' all. Plus, you're our best player after me and Les and Gus. Heh, heh!" The two of them laughed heartily.

It was clear Tim had forgotten something important. Yes, tonight was Wednesday, which was—why, yes, his bowling night! Some time ago Betty had talked him into joining the bowling team, though he wasn't much enthused. He did sign some paper, which he didn't really read because he wanted to get it over with. Apparently that contained a clause or whatever about what happens to the wife of a player when that player missed a certain number of games in a row, perhaps as few as two.

Upstairs, Betty shrieked, giggled and laughed. The happy sounds bothered Tim more than the shrieks did. He began to wonder why he didn't go upstairs and put a stop to it. He didn't seem to have the will. Perhaps it was because of that paper he'd signed. An agreement was an agreement, after all. It may not be legally binding, but ethically . . .

"How many team members are there?" He couldn't recall.

"Whaddya mean, how many? Just us four, including you," said Les. "Standard bowling team. What, you wish there was more?"

Les and Bill finished up their sodas and went back upstairs. Tim sat in his usual chair in the living room and, finding the re-mote at an end table, pressed the button to turn on the TV. What came up was an image of a record player, playing what appeared to be a partially melted and broken record that produced the same repeating cawing sound coming from upstairs. He punched the remote repeatedly, but the same image was on every channel.

After some time, Tim woke in his armchair. The TV was buzzing like a hornet, and the sound wasn't coming from upstairs anymore. He got up, pulled aside the curtains and peeked out the window, seeing there were no cars in front of the house anymore. He went upstairs, finding Betty still in bed, quiet and alone.

"Betty, get up. We need to talk."

"Really, Tim," she said, "I'm exhausted. Can't get up now."

"Betty, I didn't want to do anything before when the fellows were here, but now I'm talking to you, and I'm not asking you, I'm telling you to get out of bed!" He fiercely pulled back the covers and tried to throw them, but they swooped low and fell flat to the floor.

Betty kept lying there with her eyes closed, clutching her pillow more tightly. "Oh Tim, I'm really tired. Won't you please just put the covers back and let me sleep?"

Tim was getting very frustrated, not just at Betty's unwillingness to obey, but at the fact she was able to do so at all. Where had his power gone? Was something wrong with the Bliss service?

"Betty, I mean it! Now get up!"

Groaning, Betty pulled herself up, blinked her eyes open and thrust her legs over the side of the bed. "OK, I'm up. What?" She yawned loudly.

Tim wasn't at all convinced Betty had gotten up because of his power over her. Her defiance suggested she'd done so of her own free will. That was bad, very bad. Tim also couldn't help but notice that Betty's legs were rather attractive, and the rest of her figure, displayed in her filmy slip, was slender and fetching. The thought of what the fellows on the bowling team had done to that body, which belonged to him . . . At the thought of it, he found himself getting even angrier than before.

"No wonder you're tired. Really exerted yourself, didn't you?" he said acidly.

"Oh, don't start. It was your bowling team. If you'd remembered to go bowling, it wouldn't have happened."

"You—how can you say that? You're just—shameless! A shameless hussy. A slut!"

Betty's eyes widened, and she fixed her gaze upon Tim. Their eyes met in a vibrant collision, but she pulled away after a few moments, put her face in her hands and began to cry.

"Betty—what are you doing?" Betty went on crying. "Don't, don't do that, I can't stand it when you cry. I'm, I'm sorry I called you that, that name. It's just that I'm upset. Understandably upset. I mean, just consider how it makes me feel . . ."

Betty stopped crying abruptly and looked up. "I'm not crying about that. I'm crying because I miss Skip." She put her face back in her hands and went on sobbing.

Tim was dumbstruck. After a minute or so of working his mouth around so that he might again form words, he croaked out, "Betty, we agreed we'd never mention that person again."

"I don't care," sobbed Betty. "I drank the sherry in the fridge when your friends came over and told me about the bowling deal. I'll say it whether you want to hear it or not. I loved Skip, so there!"

Suddenly Tim was truly furious. "So . . . so you loved him, despite all he did to you. Drank like a fish! Took you for granted.

Went out with other women. Slapped you around, even. Yes, I'll say it, I'll say it because it's true!"

"So will I. I loved Skip! He had his faults, but he loved me and showed it. I don't care what else happened. I'll say it, because it was true. He was sweet and kind," she sniffled, "most of the time."

"Oh, yes, sweet and kind! Do you actually think he cared anything about you? He didn't care about anyone but himself. Couldn't even hold a job. And love? He couldn't love anyone. He even admitted it! He knew what a heel he was—and that he wasn't good enough for you! That's why he left. And you agreed that it was for the best, and said you were glad!"

Sobbing more, Betty admitted, "Yes, I said that."

"So let me get this straight . . . despite me breaking my back to provide a decent home for you and the children, despite all the real love I've shown you, you still would rather have Skip mistreating you. You, you actually prefer him to *me*! Is that what you're saying? Is it?"

Betty sighed, pulled her legs back into the bed, reached over to the lamp table and picked up a pack of cigarettes Tim hadn't noticed there before. She took one out, lit it up. Tim was aghast.

"When did you start smoking?"

"Started again. I started smoking *again*."

"Betty, don't you know those are just terrible for your health, and a very poor example to set for the children? It's also a fire hazard!"

"Oh, for Christ's sake," she said, suddenly furious. "When I married you, I didn't know I was marrying a, a *mutant*! And I can't put up with this stink anymore!"

"Stink?" Tim was horrified. "What do you—"

"The stink from you!" said Betty. "Don't pretend you don't smell it. You bring it home from work and it's all over this house!"

She put out the cigarette on an edge of the bedstead, rolled onto her belly and wrapped the pillow around her face.

"But, Betty, what the—why didn't you ever—"

"Go 'way, leave me alone," she muttered into the pillow. "Jus' lea' me alo'."

Tim flapped his arms in exasperation, turned and walked out of the bedroom. The stink from me, he thought. Ridiculous!

He hurried down the steps and plopped down in his armchair. Great, just great! Now things were so out of control she was even bringing that reprobate Skip up! Some assurance policy! He should call those people up tomorrow and . . .

No, no, what was he thinking? He couldn't, wouldn't dare cancel the policy. But he would have to call them, try and find out what was wrong, what he could do to set it right again. He felt everything falling, the world crumbling beneath his feet, but he mustn't give way, mustn't let himself think so negatively about things that didn't do any good, that only made him feel worse. That might even be the main thing that's wrong, his negative thoughts, which lingered in the back of his mind even when he tried to shut them out. He closed his eyes and pleaded, with himself, with a higher power, with his evil thoughts themselves: Please, please leave me in peace! All I want is a little peace and comfort. Just a little happiness. A little . . .

He thought to call out and ask for a fudge bar, but in great exasperation, and then sorrow, he realized he'd have to go to the kitchen and get it himself.

4.

When Tim arrived at work the next day, he was preoccupied and worried about Betty, as well as about the fact he hadn't done any work at all the day before, having spent the entire day with Drivel and his girls. The whole business with Drivel and the seashore wouldn't have happened if he hadn't gotten lost on his way to work. How would he explain this to Mrs. Henderson?

He still wasn't sure how to get to his office by way of the elevators and decided he'd better take the stairs. Doing so, he found that though the stairs led upward, while stepping up them he had the strangest sense of being upside down, so if he didn't step down heavily, it felt as though his feet might not make it all the way to the stairs.

Exhausted and confused, he dragged himself out of the stairwell to see Nan waiting by the elevator banks, without knowing what floor he was on. The doors opened and, as Nan was stepping forward into the elevator, she turned to look at him and tumbled downward with a piercing scream.

Tim ran over, looked into the elevator and saw it was an empty shaft. He tried to look down it, but the elevator door began to close. He barely pulled his head out in time.

He ran back to the stairwell and hurried up the next flight, again feeling he was upside down and having a hard time keeping his footing and finally had to grab the edge of the entrance to the next floor as the stairway beneath him seemed to fall away. If only Mr. Drivel were there to pull him up as he had been the day before!

As he struggled, an elevator door appeared and closed before the entrance, and Tim let go in alarm, falling.

He thought he was going to die, but the fall turned out to be short. Landing in a neck-deep pool of water at the bottom of an elevator shaft, he expected to find Nan there, alive or dead, but instead, the girls from yesterday emerged, smiling and laughing as they converged upon him, twisting flowers into his hair, playfully dunking him and naughtily putting their hands down the front of his pants. As they swished their long tails, he realized they had again become fishy-smelling mermaids.

As he was half-heartedly fending off the mermaids and feeling the first perks of the savage hunger that had beset him the day before, the floor of the shaft rose to the level of another elevator door, which opened, and Tim, the girls and most of the water were dumped out. The girls' tails faded quickly, they again developed legs and, still giggling, ran away.

Dazed and soaked to the skin, Tim saw, with some relief, he was on the 6th floor. Though still a bit hungry, he suppressed his urge, and was glad there hadn't been an incident just then.

He stumbled into his office and came to his cubicle and saw to his great surprise his terminal was gone. Walking down the aisle of cubicles, he saw all the terminals were gone.

There were other employees about, but not at their desks. Everyone seemed to be assembled around the Space Saver, talking in low, fretful voices. Drawing nearer, he saw the machine had changed drastically and was now a red, gelatinous mass, still more or less in the shape of the old Space Saver. It seemed to be quivering, slightly but very rapidly. Tim's co-workers appeared to be curious about it, but reluctant to get very close.

"Are we sure it's the same one?" asked Willa.

"It is, it's just changed. It's definitely getting bigger," said Marjorie.

"I think it's creepy," said Willa.

"How are we supposed to do our work," asked Sue, the only one among them who seemed indignant about the changes that had taken place, "with no terminals?"

"Now, Sue," counseled Mrs. Henderson, "I'm sure when Mr. Grovel comes in he'll have some instructions for us. Apparently this is part of the renovation project we were told about."

"Nobody told us about this!" said Sue. "This is all you-know-who's doing! When is Mr. Grovel going to put his foot down about all this foolishness? He's supposed to be the department head!"

"Now, let's just be calm," said Mrs. Henderson, though she seemed a bit shaken herself. "I think we should all return to our desks. As you see, the files are available, so—"

"But *how* are they available? I want to know whether I'm still in that thing or not!" said Sue, pointing accusingly at the red mass.

Renner, who'd been lingering quietly some distance away while the others were around the Space Saver, now dashed forward and ran his finger into the red goo it had apparently become, scooping up a dollop and putting it in his mouth.

"Ewww, gross!" said Marjorie, at which Renner grimaced, showing red-stained teeth, and scurried away.

Feeling dazed and a little nauseated, Tim crept back toward his desk as Mrs. Henderson had suggested.

His co-worker Pat, a wan, usually silent girl with a faint mustache, turned in her seat as he staggered past her. "You're all wet," she said. "Is it raining out again?"

Tim turned, stared at her for a moment, and said, "What happened? Where's all the terminals?"

"You weren't here yesterday, were you? The midgets and dwarves were both here together, and took them all away! That's all everybody's been talking about."

"What did they tell us about how we're supposed to work?"

"They didn't. But you can get the files. The filing cabinets are right where they always are—across the hall—and all the files are in there. You just don't have to put your head in your terminal anymore. I like it better this way. Hey, you've got a flower stuck in your hair."

Tim brushed the remaining flower away. He thought about the rumor Nan had told him about before, that they'd just be in the Space Saver all the time without having to turn it on. And what had Drivel said was going to happen?

Tim said, "But are we—are we still having the PQI workshop today? It is today, isn't it?"

"Oh yeah, sure," said Pat. "That should be fun." She smiled, showing a row of tiny front teeth accented with metal braces.

Back at his desk, Tim tried to look through some of the files he found there, but was too distracted to be able to focus on them at all. He considered whether he should say something about Nan having fallen down the elevator shaft. But had she really done so? Maybe he had, well, imagined some part of that. He was beginning to wonder if his perceptions weren't getting maybe a little untrustworthy. The appropriate person to speak to about Nan would be Mrs. Henderson, but he didn't really want to approach her because she might ask him where'd he'd been the day before.

"Hey everybody, where's Nan?" he heard Marjorie say, but no one answered.

It seemed to Tim the Smell was especially unpleasant that day, like the odor from a pile of wet clothing allowed to grow mildewed. Maybe when they finally took down the walls they'd find some longstanding dampness within them.

After pretending to work for what only seemed a moment, Tim had a sense he was alone in the room. He looked up to see the room was again empty. Why, everyone had gone to the workshop without him!

He jumped up and ran into the hallway and felt, to his surprise, something bump up against the back of his knees. He turned, and at first it appeared to be a large, three-dimensional blue spot, but he realized, as it went on nudging him, it was a floating, inflated chair he was supposed to sit down in. He did, and the chair whizzed forward, zig-zagging through several corridors. Soon Tim was relieved to see some of his co-workers, floating ahead of him in similar inflatable chairs, some also blue, and others red or yellow.

Well, this way he didn't have to worry about finding where the workshop was held.

They arrived at the large meeting room where the PQ workshop was to take place. The room was crowded with Tim's co-workers from several different departments. Everyone was sitting in a floating chair like the one that had picked up Tim. The chairs appeared to be made out of plastic and inflated with some gaseous substance, perhaps, he thought, helium. He noticed also they floated at varying levels; several of the female staff members had weight problems, and the chairs they were in were hovering rather close to the floor, while others, including Dora and Pat, had risen quite near the ceiling. Even so, the chairs did not float about the room, but remained in stationary rows, though aloft. Mr. Renner, whose chair floated at about mid-level, had one leg pulled up at an unnatural angle, his bared foot close to his face and seemed to be preoccupied with chewing on his toes. There were a few empty chairs floating and bobbing gently in the back of the room.

A moment later, Mr. Drivel appeared in the air at the front of the room and somersaulted to his feet, ending in a pose that seemed to suggest great dignity, perhaps in part because he was now dressed in a long white robe and, incongruously, a tall black stovepipe hat. At his side, nuzzling his ear, was a giraffe.

"Hello, my dear colleagues," he began. But at that moment the room began to shake, all of the chairs in front of Tim spinning about in a frenzy as their occupants screamed. The roof of the building flew off, and as if caught in a whirlwind, his co-workers all rose up into the sky, higher and higher, until they were no longer visible and their screams became faint before no longer being heard at all.

Looking around, he saw no one was left in the room except for himself and Mr. Renner.

The room became black, and Tim thought at first he had fainted. But then a light came up at the front of the room where Mr. Drivel had been standing, and a line of happy, leggy chorus girls appeared—the same, Tim suspected, as he'd seen yesterday at the beach and this morning in the elevator shaft—in silver-spangled top hats and tails, net hose and stiletto heels, carrying straight canes to accentuate their strutting and high kicks. Drivel came out behind them at the end of the line, dressed in a baggy suit and straw boater, comically imitating the kicks done by the dancers.

"Welcome to the Bureau of Verification's first-ever PQI workshop!" shouted Drivel. "Those letters stand for Perpetual Quality Improvement! And what's our strategy, ladies?"

The girls began to answer him in succession, and each one that spoke struck an especially fetching, if not brazenly risqué, pose.

"Drive out indecisiveness!"

"Break down all barriers between sections and departments!"

"Institute a vigorous program of self-improvement!"

In unison, grasping their canes horizontally in both hands: "Re-evaluate all procedures from top to bottom to eliminate paradigmatic stagnancy! Break out of that old stale paradigm! *Think outside the box!*"

Giggling naughtily, they chanted "Outside the box, outside the box!" as they scurried off behind the stage's curtain, dragging out from there a huge white box. The box's lid flew open, and a gigantic round and yellow smiling emoji symbol emerged, its mouth opening joyfully, exposing at first a red tongue and then a tremendous, vomit-like flood of stars and rainbows that filled the meeting room.

Now floating next to him, Renner chortled and clapped happily. "Outside box, outside box!"

Somehow, amid the cacophony and chaos, Tim heard a phone ringing. The sound seemed to be within his head. Stranger still, the ring of the phone took on the quality of Betty's voice. He leapt down from his chair and walked out of the meeting room, intent, for some reason, on answering the phone. He had a sense this was an important call and had to do with his situation at home.

The ringing became a shrill, distorted voice, even more like Betty's, that seemed to be saying "Fire! Fire! The house is on fire!" His quick walk became a run, and he found himself back in his office where a red phone on his desk was ringing. He grabbed the phone's headpiece and put it to his ear, but by the time he did it had stopped ringing, and he heard from it only a loud gargling dial tone, like a death rattle. The phone seemed to be made of a sticky substance that melted in his hand, and he realized it was the same stuff as what the Space Saver had become.

The racket coming from far down the corridor where the workshop was taking place grew louder. Tim ran for the stairway, tumbling down several flights, one after another, in his rush to reach the street. He did and, with battered limbs aching, made a mad dash home.

Tim arrived at his house and found a large firetruck parked on his front lawn. The house, however, looked normal, except the front door was open. He stepped inside, said, "Betty? Betty, where are you?" He heard the voices of two or more people speaking in low tones, none of them sounding like Betty. It occurred to him burglars might be present, and his first impulse was to run away, but he remembered Betty and the twins might be in the burglars' clutches. He stormed into the next room. There he saw two firemen, each hefting one end of the aquarium that contained Clark and Shirley. Both firemen wore disgusted expressions on their faces. They glanced at him but didn't speak as they carried the aquarium past him.

Tim was about to intervene when he saw Shirley and Clark's arms and legs had become long, plantlike tendrils, complexly woven together, and their eyes as wide and empty as those of expensive tropical fish. They did not appear to see him. The water in the aquarium had turned a light, somewhat murky green. "One side, this damned stinkin' thing is heavy," a fireman said. Some of the water sloshed out onto him as the workmen went past. It felt slimy and smelled quite bad.

One of the firemen, the one who had not spoken before, came back in and thrust a clipboard into his face, a swatch of dog-eared papers clipped to it. "Need a signature, bub," he said, handing Tim a pen. Tim began to read the first page, but the words on it were out of focus and in very small print. "C'mon, c'mon, don't have all day," said the fireman. Cowed, Tim scribbled his name on the indicated line.

He went to the front door and watched the firemen climb into the truck, where they had apparently taken the aquarium, and drive away. They started using the siren once they were about a block down the street.

He turned around. "Betty," he called out, "where are you? What happened? Was there a fire? They took the twins!"

There was no answer.

Tim saw no sign there had been a fire at all, he thought, until he looked at the TV set. He saw a hole in the center of the screen, nearly round but burned around its edges, from which dark smoke wispily emerged. On top of the TV was a large manila envelope of a type they used at work. Was it a note from Betty?

The envelope, he found, was sealed. With dread, he tore it open and shook out three smaller, unopened business-sized envelopes that fell to the floor. He bent and picked them up and saw the return addresses bore, at the top, the Bliss Assurance logo. One was marked 'Late Notice' in large blue letters and the other, in still larger red letters, 'Final Notice.' He shook the envelope again, and two more envelopes spilled out: the last two payments to Bliss, with Tim's return address. Unsent, and without stamps on them, even.

The bills! Betty had been hiding the Bliss bills! That must be why he'd been having all this trouble lately!

He sat down on the sofa, dismayed, and was only there for a moment when it began to shudder beneath him, and the other furniture in the room began to shake as well, as if coming awake after a long, unpleasant sleep. The sofa began slowly to walk, heading toward the still-opened front door. Tim leaped off to see the rest of the furniture—his armchair, the coffee table, the glass cabinet filled with his collection of Pez dispensers—all tumble over with a great crash before lumbering out the door one by one. He heard steps coming from the upper floor, and down the stairs, sideways, came the bed, followed by the dressers and lamp tables. They followed after the living and dining room furniture, as if in a caravan. Tim went again to the door and watched the line of furniture ambling down the center of the street at an even ace. The neighbors, he fretted, would think they hadn't paid the bill on the furniture either. Though that, obviously, was the least of his worries.

Only the TV set was left of all his household furnishings, and it had a smoking hole in the center. He had the strange thought his head just might fit into that hole, and if it did, maybe he could find an answer as to why ... He got on his knees and leaned forward, but the thick smoke made him gag and gasp for breath. He thought he could see something just past the hole, some small, dark object. Gingerly, he reached his hand inside, found something hard and cold, pulled it out.

He gasped. It was a gun! A revolver! It even had bullets in it. But he'd never owned a gun.

At that discovery, he began to hyperventilate. The more he did so, the more a truly vile stench seemed to rise all around him, as if from an open grave—or at least, what he assumed an open grave might smell like. He looked at his hands, saw they were dingy, damp, and the skin on them was peeling away.

Caught up in a revelation, he ran up the stairs, to the bathroom, and gazed at his image in the mirror. He saw a corpse. This, he realized, was the real source of the Smell, the essence of the Smell, the ultimate Smell all the secondary odors distorted and hid. The Smell of his own rotting flesh. He was *dead!*

Knowing now he was a corpse and there was no further point in any sort of human endeavor, Tim ceased all effort, falling to the floor and remaining there in a heap for some hours until, very late that night, the phone rang. He answered it with a hoarse, whispered "Hello."

"Hello?" came the feminine voice at the other end. "Is this the Timothy Plummet residence? This is Dora, Mr. Grovel's secretary at the Bureau. Mr. Plummet?" she said, beginning to sob, "I hate to bother you, but something happened at work today after you left, and I just, I have to talk to someone. I wonder if you could . . ."

Within minutes, Tim was riding the faster of his two horses bareback across town to Dora's apartment. On the way there, he nearly had a collision with an apparently wild and deranged, if not rabid, giraffe, which charged right at him and the horse with white foam spuming from its jaws, leaping over them and dashing onward in a great frenzy.

Dora opened the door, wearing a bright red kaftan, her expression sad, a sour hint of alcohol on her breath. "Timothy, thank you for coming. Come in, please."

Tim nodded and stood inside the door, looking all around without saying anything.

"Um, please sit down, anywhere. Would you like a cup of tea or anything? Some wine?"

"No, thank you." Tim sat in an armchair.

"I'm having some, you see. I ordinarily don't, I'm just, I'm very upset." She swayed on her feet. "What you must think of me, calling you and then being like this, in this state."

"I'm glad you called, Dora."

She sat on a sofa across from him and began at once to talk rapidly. "It was so terrible, Timothy, I just can't believe what happened. Ned, I mean Mr. Drivel—there was an accident at the party today, after you left, and he, he died." Her face twisted unpleasantly and she wept.

Tim clasped his hands, waiting quietly for her to go on.

"He . . . I'm sorry"—she pulled a long lock of her hair behind her ear—"he had been getting pretty carried away, he sometimes would when he was clowning. You know how he always tried to cheer people up. It was a little hard to believe what I was seeing, it was like a dream, except I never have dreams hardly, and not . . . not like that."

Tim nodded, waiting for her to go on.

"He did this . . . this thing with a giraffe. At first he was riding it. I wasn't even sure it was a real giraffe."

"I did see the giraffe," said Tim.

"He said, 'Who wants to be first to play our game? It's like pin the tail on the donkey, only *you are the tail!*' And he grabbed up Sue, who started screaming. I thought it was a joke, a magic trick or something they'd arranged to do, though I know Susan and Ned generally don't have much regard for each other."

He took a sip of her drink.

She continued, "Anyway, he pulled out this jar . . . I didn't know jelly even came in jars that big. It got bigger, too."

"He had a jar of jelly?" asked Tim.

"Yes, red jelly. Maybe it was cherry. It was so big. The jar, I mean." She sat down and looked earnestly into Tim's eyes, as if pleading with him to understand how big the jar had been. Her eyes were very blue. "And then he . . . somehow, Susan's clothes were gone, or seemed to be, and he spun her around in this jar . . . it had become so big she fit into it! And then he took Susan, who was all covered with red jelly, and he, well . . ." She seemed reluctant to speak. "He stuck her inside the giraffe."

Tim was uncertain what she meant. "Inside?"

"Inside the back of the giraffe. You know, his . . . his heinie."

"I see."

"Head first, so you could hear her making noises in there, but they were muffled." She shuddered. "But the giraffe didn't like it either, and was making a screeching noise and dashing all over the room!

"So, when Susan was put inside the giraffe, Ned—I mean, Mr. Drivel—was laughing, but everyone else was really upset, and started to run for the exits. And when they did, Ned somehow . . . well, he grew a lot of arms! It was like an octopus, or one of those Hindu gods. At first there were four arms, then eight, then I guess sixteen, then more and more, and they stretched way, way out all over the room, and he was grabbing everyone out of those floating chairs they were in, and then he . . . Well, he was juggling them, like they were ten pins! And while he did, his mouth kept growing wider and wider, as if he was going to . . ." She seemed unable to finish.

"I see," said Tim. "This juggling, and so forth. Did he do this with you?"

"No, somehow he didn't notice me. In a funny way, it was like I wasn't even there. But then, as this was all happening, the empty chairs all changed into, just . . . spots."

"Spots, eh," said Tim. He wasn't surprised.

"And, and they all sprouted these little mouths with jagged teeth, and they just . . . they ate him!" She sobbed, put her face in her hands and was silent for a long moment, her shoulders heaving. "There was so much blood!"

She threw her hands down, again looked Tim in the eye. "But, but you know what he did while they were eating him? He laughed! Laughed like it was fun! But in just moments, he was all gone!"

"What happened to the giraffe?"

"I think it ran out of the room. But Timothy, the thing is, I think I fainted, and when I got up, I went back to the office and, everyone was all ruffled up, but they didn't . . . they weren't up-set and they didn't say anything about it!"

"Umm, hmm," said Tim.

"Timothy, do you think it was a dream? Am I crazy? It was so real!"

"I wouldn't like to speculate, Dora."

"Timothy, there's another reason why I called you. You're signed up for the Bliss Assurance plan, aren't you? Mr. Grovel said you were."

"Yes I am, Dora."

"I am too. I just joined. I didn't tell Mr. Grovel because he doesn't approve of it, but Ned . . . Ned told me I should join, be-cause it was going to become mandatory pretty soon anyway, and if I did I could, I could help him."

"I see," said Tim. "Not that it matters."

"Not that it . . . I'm sorry?"

"I just mean it doesn't matter to me," said Tim.

"You don't . . . you don't care that Ned—that Mr. Drivel—was killed?"

"No, not at all. Though I can empathize with Mr. Drivel, be-cause my own situation is, in fact, the same as his."

She stared at him dumfounded. "But what do you—"

"You see, I'm dead too," he explained calmly. "I have been for some time, though I just recently came to realize this."

Her face was a blank slate. Then she laughed, suddenly and loudly; a despairing laugh, he thought. It ended abruptly.

"Don't say that," she said, in a voice so low it was nearly a whisper. "It's not nice, and it's creepy."

"It's not that I don't wish to care, Dora. You must understand that. I wish to care a great deal, because I know how this upsets you, and I wish to care for you very much. Even now, strangely enough."

"But you're . . . married," she said.

"Well, Dora, it is true I'm married, but in fact, my wife has recently left me. Which I suppose I can't blame her for, considering I'm dead."

"Stop saying that!" she sobbed. "It's not you who's dead, it's Ned! I watched him die!"

"I'm sorry to hear about Mr. Drivel's death, Dora, if that does turn out to be the case, but I must insist I'm deceased as well." He paused. "Well, I guess I shouldn't say I'm sorry, because I'm really not, I suppose. I feel as though I am sorry, but it must be a delusion. As a dead person, it shouldn't be possible for me to feel anything. And besides, we're all going to be in the Space Saver eventually, and when you're there, it doesn't matter whether you're dead or not. Time doesn't matter, and neither does space. It's quite different from the way it is outside. You were smart to go with the Bliss plan, though. It really makes the whole experience of the Space Saver much more fulfilling."

"You're making fun of me, aren't you?" she said. "You're acting crazy because you think I'm crazy."

"You probably are, but that doesn't matter either."

"Why did I call you? Go away, please."

"Of course I'll go, if you want me to. I'm sorry, I mean, I would be sorry if—"

"Just go!" She threw herself face down on the couch, sprawled across it, her kaftan rode up to reveal a great deal of her very attractive right leg. The leg, in fact, was clothed in a sheer dark stocking, fixed to a garter, which continued up higher beneath er clothes.

Tim stood watching her for some moments, as she lay there weeping, studying her fetching form as he had, indiscreetly, so many times at the office. Somehow, in fact, her weeping made her even more appealing, in a way that seemed alien to Tim, or at least, unexplored. If he were alive, he knew he'd never allow himself to do what he now found himself inclined to do. He would never, ever, in fact, have done something so reprehensible, so absolutely criminal, so very . . .

Tim leaped unto Dora, knocking over and extinguishing the end table lamp in doing so. She struggled and cried out futilely in the dark as Tim tore away her garment and ripped off her left leg and began to devour it, growling with pleasure.

5.

Tim arrived for work somewhat early the next morning with a distracted look about him and an oddly incongruous determination in his step. He had no trouble getting to his office, flying up the flights of stairs to the 6th floor as easily as if he were riding a set of unusually fast escalators.

Once upstairs, he walked past Mr. Grovel's office without even glancing into the door, though once past it, he wondered whether Dora was in yet.

He went into his office. He didn't glance at the little group of his co-workers who were already at their desks, chatting before the workday began. They didn't seem to notice him much, being engrossed in a conversation about a fresh local news story, something about a parolee who'd robbed a carryout run by Arabs whom, as everyone knew, would shoot anyone at the drop of a hat, as they indeed did in this case, though the miscreant wouldn't have been out on the street anyway if it wasn't for all those soft-hearted liberals on parole boards, and so who could blame the Arabs, even though they had no business being over here in our country taking Americans' jobs. Are they soft-hearted or soft-headed, said someone, to titters of amusements, which increased to loud laughter when someone said something ribald about being soft. But, Tim reasoned, he had no way of knowing whether they were really there and even if they in some sense were, it made no difference now.

The Smell was quite putrid, but now that he understood what the source of it was, he accepted it as a matter of course.

He was surprised they weren't talking about Mr. Drivel's death. Maybe, he thought, it didn't really happen and Dora had simply imagined it. Of course, it all depended on how she had gone about imagining it and whether she had been the only one to do so.

His desk was empty, but he decided he would prefer it to be full of file folders, rather than having to retrieve them from the files. At that thought, large piles of folders appeared on his desk—more than he'd wanted, actually. He made a note to re-member to be more careful. But then, what difference did it make, now that he was dead?

He picked up the nearest folder, opened it and studied it intently, glancing at the words in succession without grasping their meaning in combination.

"Where's Sue?" he heard someone ask, but there was no answer.

As he continued looking through the files before him, however, he became a bit irritable. He would snatch a file folder from the top of the pile suddenly, lay it open before him and stare at some of the words for some time, as if waiting for them to change somehow, so they would at once make sense. It was as though he were waiting for a cocooned larva to burst forth as a lovely multicolored butterfly, or at least as a gray moth. That is, as if he expected something quite interesting to happen at any moment and didn't want to miss it.

For a while after that he held very still, concerned any movement on his part might disturb the process he was observing. But quite abruptly he would turn the page, yank his hand away as if stung, and then go on staring in stillness as before.

He sensed, or perhaps saw out of the corner of his eye, someone was approaching. It was Willa, striding toward his desk and looking right at him.

Tim pretended not to notice her, just in case she really was there. Apparently she felt she was because she came up and said, "Tim, do you still have those files for Manning Hardware, the company that hadn't reapplied for Fund Assessment for the last three years or whatever it was? Majorie said yesterday you had them last Thursday."

"No, I'm sorry. I do not," said Tim. He rubbed his fingers against the revolver he'd brought from home, which was in his suitcoat pocket.

"By the way," she added, giving Tim a direct look over her glasses, her voice hushed, "Isn't it just terrible about poor Nan Sputner? You heard, didn't you? They found her at the bottom of an elevator shaft in the basement. People say she drank, you know. You used to work with her, didn't you?"

"Yes, I did work with her. No, I know nothing about it."

"You mean you didn't know about the drinking, or about the

accident?"

"I know nothing about any of it," he said. He didn't mean to be snippy, but apparently he sounded that way, because she scowled, turned on a heel and walked back toward her desk. Tim remembered to ask, after she was some distance away: "But what about Mr. Drivel?"

He must have spoken loudly, because several people looked up.

"What about him?" asked Willa.

"Is he still . . . here?"

"What do you mean, still? He usually doesn't get in 'til 9."

How odd, mused Tim, that none of his co-workers, at least none of those present, seemed to have been impressed by the colorful occurrences at the PQI workshop the day before. Stranger still was the fact they didn't even notice that he himself was dead.

There came a loud crushing sound.

"They're taking down the walls down the hall," said Willa. "With sledgehammers. Those little guys can pack a punch."

As he continued leafing through the folders before him, some strange thoughts passed through his mind. Some took the form of visions, vivid pictures appeared suddenly, froze, and flew away in a blur, bending out of shape as they spun into the distance, distorted by the speed of their departure. He saw Dora's face, at first pretty and stern as she had always been at the office, but then sad, like a little girl about to burst into tears, then her mouth opened wide, much too wide, as though she saw something that terrified her to a supernatural degree. Her mouth stretched and stretched until it filled Tim's field of vision, and her beauty turned grotesque, with only her sad blue eyes retaining their allure.

Though he did not see them—and wouldn't look around him, fearing to do so—he sensed his co-workers lingering near, as phantoms. He was careful not to make any sound or movement that might attract their attention. No, he had fooled them, he decided, by pretending to be absorbed in his work. In fact, he was pretending so well the words on the papers before him were on the verge of drawing his attention enough to become legible. . .

After some moments of this, he came to a sudden point of sharp awareness, realized he'd been seeing things that weren't really there. A wave of irritation passed through him, as if he'd caught himself daydreaming when he had much work to do—which in fact, was currently the case. Furthermore, it was always the case! At this thought, he began tapping his pencil with what seemed to be impatience.

Pencil? Where'd he get a pencil? The long slender object in his hand, pencil or no, began sprouting green fuzz as he studied it, like a chia pet. He shook it, and the fuzz fell off. This nonsense wouldn't happen if he'd stop daydreaming, darn it!

His movement must have made a sound for, at once, Mrs. Henderson was standing near, and glanced over at him, distracted, frowning. Tim caught her gaze and returned it for a clogged, bloated and stifling moment in time. Finally, her mouth opened and he winced, anticipating it might expand hideously, but it did not, and her tone was oddly sympathetic.

"Timothy, is there something wrong?"

There was a long pause before Tim responded. In fact, he broke his pause only reluctantly. This hesitation for the sake of hesitation seemed to peeve Mrs. Henderson a bit.

"Excuse me, Tim, but are you pausing for some specific reason?"

"Why, no," said Tim, "not at all."

"Good, very good," she replied. "Now, don't you have any work to do? I'm sure we can find some for you if you don't."

Tim muttered apologetically he did indeed have some work to do, thank you, of course, right away, thank you.

A sound of hammering machine-gun fire and faint screams were heard. "Claimants getting out of control downstairs again," someone commented.

Feeling self-conscious and dazed now, under Mrs. Henderson's disapproving eyes—wait, were her eyes still there? He could feel them, but didn't dare to look. He gathered up all of his files in his arms, quite a bunch of them in fact, and shaking off the residue of those unpleasant visions he'd just experienced, walked as unsteadily as a novice drunkard across the room to a row of file cabinets. Why hadn't he zipped rather than walked, done a somersault or two? No, too shaky, and might have drawn attention anyway. Prudence, always better to be prudent.

He had only a vague notion of what he was about to do. He was surprised when his intent, his need, his duty rose to the forefront of his mind.

Indeed, something, not quite a voice, was beginning to exert its will over him, to tell him what to do and to do it now. After all, he was not a supervisor himself, and at this point he especially needed someone to tell him what to do, he being dead and all. The voice couldn't be Mrs. Henderson's, however, since she didn't even know about his condition. Besides, it didn't sound like her, though he couldn't exactly hear it, really, it was just here.

It told him, quite clearly if not in words, exactly, to open a certain file drawer and to drop a certain file, one buried among all those collected in his arms, into a particular drawer. He wasn't sure the voice was right, but perhaps it wouldn't matter since the files weren't real, they were just an illusion produced by the Space Saver—but where would they be once the Space Saver was turned off? But perhaps it would not be turned off, so once again, it wouldn't matter if it turned out to be a mistake.

The command as to where to drop a certain file had, Tim noticed, nothing whatever to do with alphabetical order, which the files did not seem to be arranged in anyway, but perhaps that was something in the SS system that needed tweaking. Once tweaked, everything should be in the right place. In a sense, the arrangement seemed an antidote to the tyranny of alphabetical order, or perhaps, a healthy rebellion against it, or at least a mildly witty comment upon it.

As he went on methodically filing, Tim wondered why he hadn't thought of doing this sort of thing before. But then, he mused, it wasn't exactly him thinking of it now, was it?

At times, it was not immediately clear where he should leave a particular file, or whether the file he had in hand really belonged, in any sense, in a drawer he happened to have opened. He caught himself almost making a mistake more than once and scolded himself for it, silently. He needed, he told himself, to pay more attention to what he was doing and not let his mind wander so. When he would find just the right spot for one and slip it in, he was filled with a feeling of contentment, as though he were sinking into a nice warm bath with plenty of time to soak, at home. Ah, home. But that was over now.

As he filed away the last few folders of the once-big pile, feeling more and more confident each was going precisely where it belonged, he began to move gracefully, artistically even, to dance back and forth along the long row of file cabinets as he worked. As he did, he reflected upon the remarkable fact, which just occurred to him as a revelation, the files would never, ever be found again, except by pure accident, for no one knew the key to his filing system, not even he. Further, he wondered whether the particular locations he'd been led to leave the files in were not, in fact, determined by the very impossibility that such an accident would ever occur.

Tim again felt the presence of a co-worker very near, and turning, he again found Mrs. Henderson quite near him, behind him and looking over his shoulder, frowning with, he assumed, suspicion. His chest tightened. Did she know?

"Timothy, we haven't heard from Sue yet today, so I suspect she may not be coming in. I see you've almost finished all your filing, so I'd like you to stamp and collate these monetary predetermination forms I was going to give her to do. They need to be completed this morning so I can pass them along to Mr. Prober."

Tim nodded and accepted the small batch of file folders from Mrs. Henderson. She squinted at him distrustfully, turned abruptly and stepped away. Tim watched her trail away, her feet just slightly above the floor, and sit down at her desk, her back to him. The desk swallowed her and disappeared.

At that, Tim zipped to his task and proceeded to file away all of Sue's monetary predeterminations in accordance with his secret system. He was glad for the chance to help clean up the mess she'd left behind.

Now having nothing at all left to do, he returned to his desk.

He sat down and folded his hands, remaining appropriately still for someone who was dead. He was oblivious to the tepid activity around him, watching the hands of the clock—my, hadn't it gotten big, filling up nearly the entire office wall!—move ever so slowly, with quiet satisfaction. Oddly, he found himself thinking about his horses. Silly creatures! Yet so loyal. Then he started thinking about cars instead. He used to have a car, a long, long time ago, or so it seemed . . .

After a while, Tim rose and stepped over to the water cooler. Pulling a cup from the dispenser, he noticed for the first time the cooler contained not water but yellow mush with blue and red globs floating in it, which his co-workers Marjorie and Willa were riding, as though they were seahorses in a magic sea kingdom. A conversation was taking place between them.

"Well, something must have happened. I mean, it's not like her at all," said Marjorie.

Willa nodded. "June said she sounded distracted and upset."

"Ha! She's always distracted. Catatonic, just about."

"But not upset, that you can't say," said Willa. "According to June her voice was all shaky, like she was trying not to bust out bawling. Wonder what's up."

"I don't know what all, but obviously it has to do with you-know-who and her. Everybody knows something's going on between those two, though God only knows what she sees in him."

"It's often the quiet, snooty ones who are the real gold-diggers, you know."

It occurred to Tim just then the water cooler, which contained yellow mush with blue and red spots floating in it, was in the same location the Space Saver had been. Why hadn't he noticed this before? Of course, it *was* the Space Saver! At this thought, his eyes filled with sentimental tears, and he patted the cooler on its top. "Old comrade," he said.

He went back to his seat and sat down.

It was funny, thought Tim, cars were really these little boxes on wheels, with people inside, rolling down the street in rows. It was like all the people were sitting still at the same time they were moving . . . all those little people in little boxes . . . like coffins, only with wheels. And you didn't stay in them forever. He didn't need a car anymore, he reasoned. He really needed a coffin. Instead of those silly horses.

Engrossed in these thoughts, Tim jounced when he felt a tapping on his shoulder.

He looked up. Once again, it was Mrs. Henderson. This time, for whatever reason, he felt no apprehension at all and only smiled at her fondly.

"Timothy, shouldn't you be doing something now?"

Tim looked her full in the face with perfect innocence. "Yes? What?"

"You should be taking your break, Timothy. Haven't you checked this week's break schedule? Will you please try to go according to the schedule, so the rest of us can as well? It's time, Timothy."

Still gazing at her, Tim shuddered slightly. This was it, the occasion he'd been waiting for. Without replying, Tim got up and headed for the staff lounge.

As he walked to that fateful chamber, he tenderly stroked the gun in his pocket. He found it surprisingly warm. It had been quite cold when he'd taken it from the TV. In its unambiguous solidness, its hardness, it was wonderfully simple and real. It was good.

And the moment he'd been waiting and hoping for for so long, the act he'd at last found the strength and, yes, the insight to accomplish, was now only seconds away as he stepped to the entrance of the lounge. The clock was ticking reliably to its climax. Tim could feel his hummingbird heart beating in his throat as he threw open the staff lounge door. However, he at once sensed something was amiss.

"Hi, Timmy! How's your day goin' for ya?" It was Mrs. Lumpkin, the housekeeper. Mrs. Lumpkin had chronic back trouble she complained about rather frequently, especially when one encountered her in the staff lounge, seated reclining at one of the tables, as she was now. She was also, just now, munching a pickle, with an open jar before her. "You want a pickle, hon? They're sweet, you might not like 'em. A lot of people don't."

This was just wrong, thought Tim woefully. Everything had felt so right. He was certain the moment had come. There shouldn't have been anyone in the room. He hadn't even considered there might be.

Mrs. Lumpkin didn't seem to notice Tim hadn't responded to her question, or he was staring fixedly at her. "My back's just been buggin' me and buggin' me today," she said, placing a hand on what was apparently the troubled spot. "I been to three different doctors in just the last month, counting the chiropractor, and they don't none of them know what's wrong with it. I was just telling Marjorie just now, it gets so I can't hardly stand up sometimes, unless I move real slow.

"And you know I don't get no sympathy for it around here from the custodial staff. The office staff, they're a lot nicer people. But that Cecil, I asked him to go around and empty those waste cans out for me this morning because I can't lift them, which is his job as much as it is mine, but no, no, he's too gosh-darned busy mopping the restrooms. Only four restrooms in the whole building, how long can it take to mop those? Takes him all morning. Big man like him. I swear, honey, I'd take some time off to get back on my feet if I could, but they all start having conniptions if I say I'm even thinking about it, the building manager does." She decisively bit off half a pickle and chewed a few moments with an inward expression.

"And that daughter of mine, that Chrissie—brings my beloved grandchildren over every time I turn around for me to babysit, don't even call first half the time, she comes over last Saturday, says it's gonna be an hour she's going to the store, has to go, leaves me stuck with those wild uncontrollable young'uns for three solid hours, and by the time I've been chasing them around I can't hardly get up out of my chair, and that Jaysey, the youngest one, he just comes up and jumps right in my lap when I've told him and told him—"

"It's time for my break, Mrs. Lumpkin," said Tim. He reached into his shirt and tore the pistol out from the bandages, raised it to his head, and pulled the trigger.

Tim found himself lying on the floor, blood fountaining out of the middle of his face, spilling over his chin, down his neck and pooling onto the floor around his head. He heard Mrs. Lumpkin talking loudly, and fast footsteps. After that, there were more voices, but softer and softer, and he saw above him more and more faces, peering down with appalled expressions. But the faces became softer as well and, becoming one with the voices, blurred away into murmurs and mist.

Some time passed in that soft blur. Abruptly, he found himself sitting in an uncomfortable chair and could hear the sound o typing nearby. He touched his nose and found a bandage there.

"Oh, there you are, hon. You feeling better now? How's tha Band-Aid? Don't bleed all over my rug, now."

"What happened?" came a man's voice, which he recognize as that of Cecil, the other custodian.

"He just fell right over on his face and smashed the hell righ out of his nose. It might be broken, but you know you can't se no broken nose."

Mrs. Henderson's face hung over him, all too close. The en larged pores in her nose were extremely large.

"Timothy, are you all right?"

"Yes, I'm fine," he said. In fact, his mind felt clearer than i had in a very long while. And he couldn't smell the Smell any more. Perhaps that was why he felt so different.

"Mr. Grovel would like to speak to you once you get to feel ing better. He's busy with someone right now, but he'll be wit you as soon as he's finished. Why don't you go to his office an wait?"

Tim touched his bandage again, which was slightly damp though the bleeding seemed to have stopped. Cecil helped hir up, and once on his feet, he wobbled off to Mr. Grovel's office.

He sat quietly in the outer room to Grovel's office, near Dora' vacant desk. Eventually he heard Mr. Grovel's voice, as h opened the door and was finishing up talking to someone. Grov el and a short bespectacled man stood shaking hands in th doorway. "Shouldn't be any problem at all, we've got 'em cov ered. You bet. Give my regards to Mr. Takashowa over there a OI."

"Mr. Takashowa?" came another voice. "Well, he's retired now, we don't see him often. He's mostly back in Tokyo playing golf."

"Oh hell, that's right. Mr. Teakettle's the man in charge there now, correct? Teawilliker?"

"Bruce No is the department head now." The fellow cleared his throat.

"Dr. No! That's it, sure. Tell old Bruce that Roger Grovel said hey."

"Certainly. Have a good day, sir." The bespectacled man walked past Tim without looking at him.

"Jesus," muttered Grovel. He stuck his head out of the door and squinted in Tim's direction. "Plummet? Still in one piece, huh? Come on into the office, we need to talk."

In the office, they sat down. "So, Plummet, what the hell is going on here? You get a nose bleed or have an accident or what?"

Tim decided not to mention the gun. "I, I'm not sure how it happened, I just kind of found myself on the floor, and my, my nose . . ."

Grovel shook his head. "First Nan and then you. Nobody knows up from down or what the hell's going on when that god-damn whatchmacallit thing is running. Well, we're stuck with it now." He coughed, shook his head again. "What the hell day is this, Tuesday? My desk calendar says Tuesday."

"Yes, it's Tuesday," said Tim.

"Could of sworn yesterday was Thursday. Jesus, Mary and Joseph. Don't know any more whether you're coming or going around this place." He put his fist to his mouth and coughed, very hard, made a gargling noise in his throat, and spit into the wastebasket by his desk.

"So, anyway, looks like you were, whatever it is, discombobulated, bleeding a little and lying on the floor and whatnot, so you're supposed to file a claim and get examined by a physician within two weeks, or whatever. Dora can tell you when she gets back. It's all covered under that program of yours. You got this special status and all, might as well get something for it, assuming you will."

"Special status?"

'Sure, you signed up for that damned program, didn't you?"

"Umm, this was about, umm, which one was it?"

"I don't even know what it's for, it's some damn . . ." He sighed. "It has to do with 'personal development,' one of those things. The attitude-changing program that OI was pushing about two years ago, it's all their baby."

"Do you mean, my Bliss Assurance policy?"

"Yeah, I guess that's the name, Bliss, that's some company they bought out. You volunteered for it, not me."

"I volunteered?"

"Sure you did, that's the only way it works. So far, anyway. Supposed to straighten out your whole life, make you think the right way to fit in. 'Course, you probably would have been canned if you hadn't, you know you were on probation and all. Pretty much hanging by a thread, as I recall. I guess it worked. You got quieter, anyway. Used to be quite a smart aleck, you know." He gave Tim a disapproving look.

"Anyway, you were the only one to sign up for it, too, so far as I know. Could have been some others later, I suppose, they don't necessarily tell me anything. Well, there's Drivel, of course, that's," he sighed, "that's a whole 'nother ball of wax, with his whole deal." He shook his head, seemed about to say more, but didn't.

"Yes." Tim was about to add something about being sorry to hear about what happened, when Grovel spoke again.

"They informed you of the problems they were having, didn't they? That leakage thing?"

"Leakage?"

"So I was told. Stuff gets all shimmery or something, and you start seeing things that aren't there. Like an ocular migraine. My wife gets those. Believe me, I've heard all about it. But they didn't send you a letter about it? Sure you've been reading your mail?"

"I, um, I do, but usually my wife, umm—"

"Anyway, I'm supposed to instruct you to call these bozos— I'm sorry, these boys—over at Bliss to arrange for the interview. They've got a building downtown. You're supposed to call them first. I've got the number right here. Oh, hell, where is it?" He looked over his desk for a minute or two, muttering. "Here it is," he said, handing Tim a scrap of paper. "You can go ahead and use Dora's phone." He looked Tim up and down. "You sure you're feeling OK?"

"Yes, I think I'm fine."

"Well, as long as you think so, you probably are. OK, I'll let you get going and make your call, I've got some stuff to wrap up here myself."

Tim thanked him and hurried out, closing the door.

After Tim got past a series of automated inquiries that required him to choose menu options, one of which was 'Bliss Assurance,' and another within that 'speak to a representative.' After a long fugue-state of muzak, a seemingly live person finally came on the phone. "Bliss Assurance, this is Andrea speaking. How can I help you?"

Tim gave his name and began to explain his situation when the woman interrupted him and asked for a registration number. Fumbling through his wallet, he found a plastic Bliss Assurance card on which the number was printed. When he gave the number, she said, "One moment," and he heard another phone ringing, and then a new voice.

"Delinquent accounts, this is Walter. Is this Mr. Plummet? Mr. Plummet, we have not received a payment from you for two months. We last received a payment on your account in September. You should have received two past-due notices and a termination notice. Your coverage has thus gone into a dormancy period of minimal protection, but I'm afraid that will expire sometime not later than the end of the month, Mr. Plummet, so this matter is critical. Your account is in arrears, is in breakdown and is facing final"—he drawled out the word—"dissolution, on . . . my goodness, today."

Tim fought to keep his voice from sounding frantic. "I haven't . . . well you see, Betty, it's my wife, she got the mail. I mean, there's been a misunderstanding. What can I do? I'll pay, I will! Anything!"

"Well, sir, you would have to come down to our main offices at the Bliss Building"—he gave the address, downtown—"and speak to someone in Delinquents, so we can arrange first to extend the dormancy, but I'm afraid that we'll be closing at 6:30 this afternoon, and it's now 5:20, so—"

"Oh, my goodness, is it that late?" He turned and looked at the clock on the wall. Its hands were moving now; the second and, in particular, with much determination. "I've got to get own there right away!"

"I'd recommend you do that, Mr. Plummet, to avoid the utter xtinction of your coverage, upon which, under your arrange- ient, your continued employment itself is conditional."

"Conditional?" said Tim.

"It would mean you'd get fired from your job," said Walter.

Tim felt as if his heart had stopped.

"And Mr. Plummet?" said Walter after some moments. "Mr. 'lummet, are you still there? I'd like to recommend that, in or- er to avoid any such unpleasantness in the future, you also sign p today for our payroll deduction plan. Oh and, yes, we'd like ou to take a survey regarding your experience, if any, of the akage problem."

Tim agreed, hung up the phone and hurried out of the office oward the elevators. God, what had he been thinking of, not igning up for the payroll deduction plan!

6.

Having just missed the bus as it went past a nearby stop, Tin huffed down the street on foot. It was getting dark, and ther were not so many people downtown because rush hour was al ready over, and the ones with office jobs were gone. There wer a few stragglers left, and most of them looked like the kind c people who didn't have jobs and who might ask him for mone. He kept his head up and avoided their eyes as he passed them b but none of them spoke to him. The thought occurred to him with a rush of shame and dread, he was like them now: no hom no furniture, a wife who drinks and smokes and no job, if h didn't get to that appointment. He put all these things from hi mind and rushed on.

He had to take control again, and the way to do that was t renew his policy. But, maybe they wouldn't even want to rene once he got there. The thought filled him with black despair. No, wait, Walter had said they would, but he had to get there in time!

But maybe after today, they'd fire him anyway, for misfiling all those files! And then for shooting himself in the staff lounge!

But wait, wait, it wasn't really that bad. Mr. Grovel had said they were going to review the whole matter. He could count on Nan to stick up for him and maintain he was a worthwhile employee, and even Mrs. Henderson might not be totally negative . . But, oh no, he'd forgotten, Nan wasn't there anymore, she fell down the elevator shaft! Sue Frisky would be the new Preverification boss, and she had it in for him—but wait, Sue was gone too, wasn't she? She disappeared along with Mr. Drivel's giraffe—and oh God, Mr. Drivel, how could he forget, Mr. Drivel was gone too . . .

Gulping, Tim decided, with an attempt at firmness, he needed to get ahold of himself. In any case, the Bliss policy was the important thing right now. He had to get it renewed. He would sign anything, *Do* anything. He would go down on his knees before them and beg, if he had to. He would crawl across the floor on his knees with his trembling hands raised in a clasp, sobbing loudly, tears streaking down his face, utterly humiliate himself and simply embarrass them into renewing his policy.

Tim noticed the next person he passed on the street, a tall unshaven man in a shabby coat, was smoking as he walked along. Without thinking, Tim stopped him, putting a hand on the man's chest. "Pardon me, could I have a cigarette?"

The unshaven man gave him an annoyed look and said, "This is my last one, pal."

"Please, let me have it," said Tim. "I haven't had one in a long time. You understand." He was pleading.

The man said, "Christ, buddy!" and gave him a hard shove.

Tim staggered backward. Watching the man walk away, he was incredulous at what he'd just done. The terrible events of the day must have unhinged him. Why, he didn't even smoke! Maybe being around Betty when she was smoking had given him a secondhand nicotine addiction. If he wanted a cigarette that badly, he'd better buy some rather than bother people on the street.

He hurried over into a carryout he spotted nearby and asked the clerk there for a particular brand, which for some reason came to mind, and for a pack of matches. As he stepped out the door, he lit one up. He coughed over his first drag but took another and began to calm down immediately.

He was still a long distance from the Bliss Building, he noted wearily. Smoking! Everyone knew it was very bad for your health. It said so right on the package! Besides, it was mostly lower-class people who smoked, and it might make a bad impression on the person at Bliss whom he'd soon have to talk to about his policy. Of course, he wouldn't smoke right in front of them—the building would surely be a smoke-free environment—but they might smell it on him. Worrying, he took a deep drag. A relaxing buzz settled over him.

But again, his thinking turned over. Maybe worrying was his whole problem. He should just be self-confident and forceful. He shouldn't let those Bliss bastards push him around. He had paid for that damn policy, until Betty started screwing around with the mail anyway, and they owed him the goddamn coverage. He would bang his fist on that Walter guy's desk and demand they renew, and if he smelled of cigarettes or even if he had alcohol on his breath, that wasn't any of their darned business.

In fact, it occurred to him, a drink right now wouldn't be bad. It might soothe his nerves a little. As it happened, he was passing a tavern just then, with a turned-off neon sign outside that said The Ruby Lagoon. It seemed kind of familiar, inviting, even.

It looked familiar inside, too. He decided to sit in a booth, didn't feel like talking to anybody at the bar. He'd just have one since he was pressed for time. The waitress came up, and he automatically ordered a double.

As he sat there taking swigs, he found himself getting more and more into a funk of anger. How the hell could Betty want that worthless Skip back? Maybe Skip had once been a person with some potential, but he never managed to get anywhere because of his negative attitude about everything. He was early on dubbed an 'underachiever' who could do fine things if he would only put forth some consistent effort, and once he'd gained that status, all the narcissistic bastard wanted to do was rest on his goddamn laurels as someone who could do better if they'd only try a little. And he could hardly even hold a job because he'd always get bored with the work, or that was his lousy excuse, anyway.

He'd certainly tried enough different lines of work: all kinds of office jobs, construction, sales, social work, it all turned out the same. He tried going to school, again and again, and sometimes did well for a little while but always screwed up and became a half-assed student by the time the term was coming to an end. He just didn't apply himself and, at bottom, was simply a lazy bastard. Into the bargain, he also felt sorry for himself over his own failures.

Tim's indignation over Skip's personality flaws rose, and he tried to wash it down with a long swig.

Plus, the goddamned guy was conceited, cynical and self-indulgent. He even aspired to be an 'artist.' Ha! Some artist! Artist at what? He couldn't draw well, really, or write, couldn't play a musical instrument to save his life, so what else was he going to do—dance?

Artist, he groused. Being an artist was just an all-purpose excuse for being an asshole, for thinking you were special and the usual rules didn't apply to you. Might work out for some people the ones who had trust funds and family money, but he sure as hell didn't. Well, maybe some of his drawings and paintings were OK, he had some skill if he'd only have developed it, but he never tried hard enough and was never satisfied with what meager works he managed to produce. Always such big plans, never any payoff. And then he'd get on his high-horse about how he wasn't willing to 'sell out' by working in some commercial field. As if the damn fool had anything to sell out! As if it was a disgrace to aim what resources you have at supporting yourself and your wife and becoming a goddamned fucking success at something, for Christ's sake!

But Betty, now, ho ho! She was always impressed with the dumb asshole, always standing up for him. Even now she was stuck on him, she'd even said so. Women—you figure 'em out!

What the fuck was so special about Skip, anyway? What did she see in him? He just always had to be different, contrary, better than everyone else. Despite all his arrogance and self-obsession, all he ever managed to accomplish was to make himself miserable, and to make Betty miserable too. She deserved better, so much better.

The drinking, too. No will power. He got Betty into drinking, oo. Like her mother said, she never drank before she got involved with that loser. Aw, fucking Christ, thought Tim, as he ossed back the last of his drink. It pissed him off just thinking bout the son of a bitch! Worthless piece of shit! God, he hated im!

Betty was damned lucky Tim had come along to save her om Skip. Betty had wanted children so badly, but Skip insisted ne world was such a fucked-up place it would be wrong to bring hildren into it. What he really thought was the whole world evolved around him, and he wasn't willing to take on any responsibility. When she finally had kids, he acted like it was all up Betty to deal with them because she was the one who wanted nem.

Well, Tim *had* taken up the responsibility of fatherhood and a ot of other responsibilities too. He'd worked his tail to the bone or Betty and those kids and what thanks did he get? She torpeoed his fucking Bliss policy, when she knew how much he needd it to keep going. Why, he'd practically sold his soul for it! No, wasn't perfect, but it was something, for Christ's sake. Sure, is job with the Bureau was still pretty awful, but at least that ay he could still have things under control at home. He could ave peace and comfort and order for once in his life. Didn't Bety want those things too? If not, why didn't she want them? Vell, it sure was all shot to hell now.

Tim thought of Clark and Shirley in the aquarium, melted ogether, their eyes gogging, their mouths going like guppies, nd put his face in his hands. Oh, God, wasn't this all just a ightmare? It couldn't be real! It was all so unfair!

The waitress was at his table again, looking at him funny. im briskly ordered another double and continued brooding. A group of people came in and sat at a booth not far from his. All of them were young men in suits and ties, except for an eye catching blond girl in a tight black dress. They were happy seemingly anyway, gregarious and laughing loudly. Tim was immediately annoyed with them, and his annoyance became much worse as he found himself listening intently to their conversation.

It was apparent from the brisk lilt of their voices that they were enjoying their own cleverness heartily. "OK, Josh, so, according to you, we need to tailor ourselves to fit into society."

Here's what I need right now, thought Tim, intellectual stimulation from some fucking college boys. Just what the doctor ordered. He wouldn't glance at them, but he kept listening despite himself.

"Please, Tyler. That isn't what I said at all. The gist of my argument is, in our culture, we've held fast and hard to ideal formed long ago, in the Enlightenment period, the American Revolution and all that, but in reality, over the course of time we've had to lower the bar more and more. This has been done to make the pursuit of happiness viable, that is, to make the object of that pursuit attainable."

The girl said, "Like Daisy Buchanan for Gatsby, only—"

A deep voice deadpanned, "Daisy today is cruising a single bar with a new diaphragm," and much hilarity ensued.

Jesus, thought Tim.

"Oh, forget Gatsby, he's so tragically nouveau riche anyway." It was Josh again, speaking authoritatively. "What we've managed to create, through the values promoted by popular culture and what we might call the technologies of social engineering, is a near-perfect world of happiness waiting for the near-perfect nincompoop to occupy it."

"My problem with this," said Tyler, "is I perceive the dark side ever creeping in, however blinded one is by visions of one's next popsicle. And even the most brainwashed or shallow of our fellow citizens can't always ignore it or explain it away. Reality will always suck in some ways. Beyond that, the swamp of the subconscious is a hard piece of real estate to drain."

"Oh ye of little faith," said Josh.

Laughter.

"You guys are so dweeby," said the blonde.

"Sure," Tyler went on, "and besides, technology doesn't fuck around. It's got its own logic. Something will develop that will make all those little annoying glitches obsolete. Humanity will need to just get in line and bend over."

"Onward the march of civilization!" said Josh, making a toast.

They all laughed gaily.

Good grief, what assholes! thought Tim. So which one will get to bone the blond chick tonight? None of them, I bet.

"Seriously, technology will solve the problem. There'll be some form of reality displacement, like television, only far more intense."

"Yes, yes," said Josh, "but remember the point is to achieve a world most people can be happy in. How that's achieved doesn't really matter. What does matter is the ultimate goal of our society is to make the world safe for nincompoops. Perhaps what we really need to perfect at this point is not the world, but the nincompoop. Homo sapiens my eye—onward the march of Homo Nincompoopus!"

Disgusted, Tim was about to get up and leave when a woman sat down at his table, across from him.

Her face wasn't really pretty, but she was young and slender and had wild red hair. Her dress, exposed by her open coat, had a low neckline. She had a nice, eye-catching smile, emphasized with dark lipstick. "Aren't they obnoxious?" she said in a low voice. "Happy idiots! They should know, huh? They sound pretty drunk to me." Tim noticed the alcohol on her own breath as she pulled a pack of cigarettes out of her purse. "Got a light?"

He pulled out his pack of matches, fumbled a light and put it to her cigarette. She smiled wider, shook her hair and said, "Thanks!" but Tim was looking past her to the clock on the wall. He shook out the match.

"Say, I hope I'm not bothering you," said the woman, still smiling, but with the slightest hint of a whimper in her voice. "It's just like, I was watching you listening to those people, and all of a sudden I thought maybe you and I were, you know, the same type. I mean that, maybe," and here she looked him starkly in the eye, "you and I could do something for each other." She looked away abruptly, took a drag off her cigarette. "But maybe it was just wishful thinking."

He studied her for a moment. He wasn't flustered, at all. She was tempting, and there had been a time when—but when? He remembered he had an appointment.

"Sorry, I have to go," he said and stood up.

She touched his arm. "Wait," she pleaded.

"You should be more careful around strangers," he said. "Some of them would eat you alive." He walked out the door of the tavern without looking back at her.

It was dark out already, and the cars had their headlights on. Maybe he'd dawdled too long. Beginning to be frightened, he stepped faster. He had to get to the Bliss Building. Why, everything depended on it! What was he thinking, stopping to get a drink! He began to run up the street, his fear rising like a sudden siren. I don't want to go back, he thought, I can't go back. I'll lose everything, everything I've worked for!

All at once the Bliss Building was before him, startling in its monumental presence. At the top of its wide beveled steps, beyond its thick-columned entrance, was a carved stone panel depicting the Bliss elk, standing before the cooling tower, a colorless rainbow looming overhead.

He hurried up the steps to the entrance. But as he reached it, he hesitated.

There was the sound of a gong, and the elk leaped away, over his head. The rainbow turned to black smoke, which poured from the tower and darkened the sky. The stench of soot hit him hard in the face. He wiped his stinging eyes, and when he took his hand away, everything had changed.

The emblem was gone. So were the stairway and the columns and the huge building that had been behind them. In their place was a structure, much smaller and shabbier, a warehouse of some kind, like many another in this rundown part of town.

He heard a kind of whining, looked around him for its source. There was nothing and no one. He turned around and walked away.

The walk back didn't seem to take nearly as long as the walk up, though he didn't hurry. There was no one else around, and the night air, full of urban fumes as it was, agreed with him, as did the distant hum of cars speeding up, leaving downtown via the freeway exits.

After walking many blocks, he realized something was wrong with his vision: everything was slightly blurred. He stopped and took off his glasses, held them a few inches from his face and looked through them. Jesus, they were way too strong. He really didn't need glasses at all, he decided.

He threw the glasses into a trash bin and stood by it for a moment, carefully peeling off his mustache, which stuck pinchingly in places. And up higher, what was this? A bandage on his nose. What was it doing there? He threw that away, too.

He strolled the last few blocks. He didn't really want to go home, but there was nothing else for him to do, nowhere he could think of that he felt like going to. Besides, he was tired. Dead tired.

When he came to the front door of his house, opened it and stepped inside, he found Betty lying on her side on the floor of the living room, her knees pulled up and her face turned down in her hands, weeping softly.

"Say," he said. She pulled her hands away, eyes widening, tears streaking her cheeks. She leaped to her feet and embraced him, sobbing. He accepted her hug, but didn't return it. Well, a little. Eventually, more than a little.

She threw her head back, her face still pretty despite her swollen eyes. She pulled her arms more tightly about his neck and sobbed again.

"I'm sorry, Skip," she said. "I wanted you to be happy, but I just couldn't stand it."

He managed to smile a little, with one side of his mouth. He believed her, and it mattered, but right then he really needed another cigarette.

Having lost a bet, Pete Risley wrote *Office Mutant* in a single sitting while attired in a full body gorilla costume minus the gloves. His previously published novels are *Rabid Child* (New Pulp Press, 2010) and *The Toehead* (Not Here Not There, 2016). His short stories have appeared in various online magazines including *Plots with Guns*, *All Due Respect*, *Pulp Metal* and *Powder Burn Flash*.

Other Grindhouse Press Titles